ALL THAT GLITTERS
IS NOT GUCCI

ALL THAT GLITTERS IS NOT GUCCI

a POSEUR novel

created by
Rachel Maude

Illustrations by Rachel Maude

poppy

LITTLE, BROWN AND COMPANY
New York   Boston

Poppy

Little, Brown and Company
Hachette Book Group
237 Park Avenue, New York, NY 10017
For more of your favorite series, go to www.pickapoppy.com

Poppy is an imprint of Little, Brown and Company.
The Poppy name and logo are trademarks of Hachette Book Group, Inc.

First Edition: May 2010

Library of Congress Cataloging-in-Publication Data

Maude, Rachel.
  All that glitters is not Gucci : a poseur novel / created by Rachel Maude. — 1st ed.
    p. cm.
  "Poppy."
  Summary: For Melissa, Charlotte, Petra, and Janie, having a Poseur handbag selected to appear in Nylon magazine's "20 under 20" fashion issue and catching the eye of Hollywood tastemaker Ted Pelligan is great, but they are determined to beat out the other young designers for the cover shot, too.
  ISBN 978-0-316-06586-3
  [1. Fashion—Fiction. 2. Publicity—Fiction. 3. Interpersonal relations—Fiction. 4. Dating (Social customs)—Fiction. 5. High schools—Fiction. 6. Schools—Fiction. 7. Los Angeles (Calif.)—Fiction.] I. Title.
  PZ7.M4368All 2010
  [Fic]—dc22

                                                                2010006407

Printed in the United States of America

Book design by Tracy Shaw

The Girl: Nikki Pellegrini
The Getup: Hot pink do-rag, spa manicure (in Chanel's "Paparazzi"), stretch denim Rihanna Romper by Black Halo, smug smile by Poseur

At Winston Prep, upperclassmen may get off-campus lunch privileges, but it's the lowerclassmen who feel seriously privileged when the high noon bell sounds its clear, Swiss Alps–worthy clang. With a confident flap of their Fendi flats (or are those fins?), tadpolers of all colors and signature Missoni stripes spill into the Main Hall and dart madly toward their destination. Because for forty-five magical minutes, give or take a few seconds, the Showroom — aka Winston's super-exclusive outdoor parking lot — was *theirs*.

Well, depending on who gets there first.

Upperclassmen popular enough to secure Showroom parking spots hop into their custom-painted Porsches and Priuses, their brightly buffed Beamers and Bentleys, and head to lunch destinations as venerable and varied as their vehicles. No sooner have the ruby taillights cleared their fine institution's Spanish colonial-style peach stucco and wrought iron gates than alert freshman from all corners of the lot swoop into the abandoned spaces. Plopping down on napkins or rarely cracked textbooks, the giddy invaders arrange brown bag lunches on the sun-baked pavement, breathing deep the lingering exhaust of their departed idols. Proximity to popularity can be intoxicating.

Unless they're just high on car fumes.

Either way, forward-thinking freshies love nothing more than popping squats in the vacant lot. Because while it's not the most *comfortable* place to eat, it *is* the most exclusive. Those who eat here today, tend to park here tomorrow . . . which is why only the *most* popular ninth-graders eat in the Showroom, banishing lesser-thans to either the sanded redwood picnic tables in the courtyard, or the lush, immaculately maintained lawns surrounding the whimsical Winston Willows, whose feathery leaves not only offer dappled shade but also protection from annoying, sandwich-seeking winged pests.

Lame.

And so it was, while mucho-worshipped sophomore Melissa Moon and devoted entourage chowed charishi chez Koi, Nikki Pellegrini, Carly Thorne, and Juliet Jackson infested her unoccupied spot and broadcasted their newfound social prowess to the world. At last, they put the C (as in *C me?*) in Nicarettes, which (as if you didn't know) happened to be the name of their clique. The three eighth-graders concocted the title one fateful day in seventh grade, combining different key syllables from each of their names. Of course, in the wake of their recently acquired high profile, haters started calling them the Dickarettes, the Moon-a-tics, and (most creative of all) "those self-absorbed idiots" — but they were just jealous.

"You know what?" Carly mused, admiring the gel-slicked blond coil plastered to Nikki's forehead. The rest of her flaxen hair had been pulled into a bun and tucked into her latest rhinestone-encrusted hot pink do-rag. "I *like* your hair this way."

"Why are you saying it like that?" gaped Juliet, majorly miffed by Carly's intonation. "You're making it sound like I *don't* like her hair this way. And I, like, love it," she insisted, spearing her boba tea with a straw. "Probably more than you do."

Oh, what a difference a month made. In one short semester, Nikki Pellegrini had swung from comparatively popular to deeply detested, then back again. Her latest surge in popularity came from cozying up to her highness Melissa Moon, who, along with fellow sophomores Charlotte Beverwil, Petra Greene, and Janie Farrish, had created her own designer fashion label, Poseur. In the last few weeks, the student-governed special study had taken on a life of its own, breaking free from its relatively humble high school origins and seizing the fashion world by storm. Or it would soon, anyway.

And of all the girls in Winston's eighth-grade class, who had the special sparkle, the commitment, the talent, the all-around je ne sais quoi, to be their honorable and estimable latte-bitch?

Which wasn't to say fetching coffee was the internship's only perk. In addition to getting first dibs on all Melissa Moon's ghetto-fabulous couture castoffs, Nikki was the only eighth-grader permitted to eat lunch in the Showroom, *and* she got to brag about it — not that she called it that. According to Melissa Moon, bragging was just another word for PR. "As in Public Relations, *not* Princess RiRi," the daunting diva quipped while Nikki had nodded, dutifully jotting the definition down. They were so bonded!

She sighed a little, now, savoring the memory.

"What?" Carly inquired, curiosity piqued by the secret smile on Nikki's face. She was always doing that . . . and it was starting to get on her not-so-secret nerves. "Why are you smiling?"

"I'm not," she coyly replied, flipping through the latest issue of *Nylon* with a Paparazzi Pink–manicured forefinger. She paused to peruse a photo, crinkling her Bioré-blasted brow. "I really hope they don't do the Poseur shoot like this. I mean, sepia?" She clucked over a color-saturated shot of Gemma Ward. "It really detracts from the high-fashion element, you know?"

Two and half weeks ago, hipster bible *Nylon* magazine had asked to feature Poseur's premier couture handbag, the Trick-or-Treater, in its 20 Under 20 fashion issue, and the photo shoot was just a few short days away. Nikki could think of nothing else.

"I guess I'll just have to keep an eye on the lighting guy, y'all," she announced with an insinuative arc of her eyebrow.

Juliet almost snarfed a boba ball.

"No way!" she gagged. "You are not going to the *Nylon* shoot. Are you going to the *Nylon* shoot? Shut. Up. No, you're not going. Are you seriously going?"

Nikki squinted her cornflower blue eyes at her possibly disabled friend. "Um, obvi. Our bag *is* being featured in the issue, y'all!" (In her tireless attempt to channel Melissa Moon, Nikki leaped at every opportunity to jam the word "y'all" into conversation. Sometimes it made sense. Sometimes it didn't.)

"Plus," she grinned. "I didn't tell you this before, but there's a *chance* we're not only going to be *inside Nylon*."

"Meaning?" Juliet furrowed her bronzer-dusted brow.

"Meaning we might make the *outside*?" She cocked an eyebrow and grinned, endlessly pleased with herself. Juliet and Carly glanced at each other, unimpressed.

"What's so great about making the outside of a magazine?" the latter scoffed, adding a roll of her bulging brown eyes for good measure. "I mean, technically *I'm* making the outside of a magazine, like, right now."

"Yeah," Juliet snorted. "What a superstar."

"You guys-uh!" Nikki slapped the pavement. "By *outside*, I mean we might make the *cover*," she elucidated, bulging her blue eyes for emphasis.

At last, she'd achieved the reaction she wanted. Her friends looked amazed and appalled — as if Taylor Lautner had revealed himself in all his bare-chested glory, only to burp in their faces.

"S'all true, y'all." Nikki sniffed, tossing her head. Her pink do-rag scintillated in the sun. "The best of the twenty designers gets to dress the cover model. And, between y'all and me? Melissa's positive it'll be Poseur."

Carly balled her fists and quivered. As if cavorting around campus with four über-popular tenth-graders weren't outlandish enough, she now got to go to photo shoots? And not just *any* photo shoot, but a photo shoot for *Nylon*, aka the coolest maggie since Gyllenhaal? She took a tiny sip of sickly tea and moistened her bee-stung lips. Now was the time. The time to tell Nikki her do-rag made her look like a sparkle penis.

Too bad Taryn Bell thwarted her plan.

"Heads up!" she screeched at the top of her lungs. As Wednesday's designated lookout, Taryn had taken her lunch perched on the Showroom's highest stucco wall, guaranteeing her a long, bird's-eye view of the winding drive that led from the Main Gate all the way down to Coldwater Canyon.

At the sound of her warning call, the lunching underclassmen paused midchew to hold their breaths, alert and still as gazelles.

"Cream-colored, mint condition 1969 Jaguar!" she bellowed.

Without missing a beat, six balletic ninth-grade girls snatched the remains of their grapes and Brie, sprang to their Miu Miu heels, and made a run for it. Barely had their frenzied frames ducked into the dim recesses of Locker Jungle than the Jaguar in question purred through the main gates. The remaining middle-schoolers swallowed and solemnly watched it pass, basking briefly in its bright, reflective light before focusing on the main event: the driver. She'd returned sporting her vintage black-sequined Chanel scarf — previously worn looped about her slender neck — as a headband, braiding the delicate silk-chiffon ends into her glossy ebony curls. On any other day, the innovation might have caused a frenzy, but as Charlotte Sidonie Beverwil cruised into the Showroom that Wednesday, there was another, even more noteworthy accessory to set admirers atwitter. Reclined into the leather passenger seat, and accentuating her style better than any belt, bangle, or bow, sat none other than Charlotte's ex-boyfriend.

Talk about retro.

"Is it true?" Juliet tilted toward Nikki and hoarsely

whispered. "Did she *really* dump Jules Maxwell-Langeais to get back together with *Jake Farrish*?"

Okay, granted: Jake had totally grown into himself over the summer. Thanks to a divinely inspired haircut and the power of Accutane, the mangy ponytail and gag-worthy pimples were things of the past. But still! Was he really supposed to compete with Jules, the half-French, half-English Orlando Bloom lookalike who, when he wasn't volunteering at nursing homes, translating Goethe from the original German, or knitting his own Henleys, zoomed around town in an acid green Ferrari? The guy wore a freaking cape! And he pulled it off! Jake had been wearing the same gray hoodie with the banged-up Amnesiac pin for, like, a *decade*.

"Look." Nikki cleared her throat. "Just 'cause she sent Euro boy packing *does not* mean she's back together with Jake. They're *so* just friends, okay? Charlotte really needs some time for herself right now."

Of course, beneath her calm and collected exterior, Nikki was on throbbing red alert. She'd been in love with Jake Farrish since, like, forever, and she wasn't going to lie: the sight of him in Charlotte's Jag put some major pain in the belly chain. Could the rumors be true? Were they back on the rocky-yet-romantic road to Jakelotte?

Crazily enough, she was the reason the pretty pair parted ways in the first place. Way back in September, on the night of Poseur's infamous "Tag — You're It" party, Nikki, who'd never so much as *tried* alcohol before, downed two flutes of champagne and ended up lip-macking Jake in plain sight of everyone at the party . . . including Charlotte Beverwil. Of course, it took Charlotte two and a half ticks to dump him, and find herself a new avowed love: making Nikki Pellegrini's life a living hell. Promptly dubbing her Icki Prostitutti, Charlotte turned the entire school (and maybe the world) against her. It took prayer, pain, and a whole lotta luck, but eventually Nikki redeemed herself. Well, Melissa Moon thought so, anyway. And if Melissa Moon thought something, so did most everybody else. Charlotte remained the one person Nikki hadn't won over, and until she did, she vowed to keep her distance from Jake. She wasn't about to wreck her ever-fragile social standing — even for her favorite future husband.

"Purple and yellow VW bus!" Taryn spat up her apple and exploded in alarm, cuing a band of semicollapsed freshman boys and girls to untangle each other from their laps and limbs and sit up, blinking with confusion. Winston's stoner royalty was returning from their daily lunchtime ritual: a jaunt to a secluded alley, followed by a trip to Baja Fresh for quesadillas, icy sodas, and endless salsa shots. Joaquin Whitman's VW bus (commonly known as the VD) rumbled through the Main Gate at a snail's pace, leaving the junior joint squad ample time to gather their flavor-blasted Goldfish and Rasta-knit hacky sacks, even in their aspiring stoner stupor. As the van creaked into its spot, neopunk sensation Creatures of Habit blasted through the grimy, half-cracked windows.

"Omigod!" Nikki wheezed, grinning madly at her friends. "Do you know why they're playing Creatures of Habit instead of Marley?"

Carly and Juliet looked at each other and shrugged (translation: they were dying to know).

"*Because* . . . Petra's dating their bassist, Paul Elliot Miller." Sighing proudly, she added, "He's the hot one."

When she wasn't sucking face with badass bassists (or bong water), Petra Greene constituted Poseur's moral center. In other words, she reminded her more superficial business partners how to be "environmentally conscious," or whatever. And sure, if all girls were born as freakishly flawless as Petra had been, then they'd probably spend their time canvassing for silkworm rights, too, *right*? But, no. *Some* people have eyelashes to curl.

Good thing Petra was super weird — otherwise the good people of Winston might die of jealousy. For now, the only people who seriously worshipped her were fellow wastoids and other such ganja groupies. As the bohemian bombshell flounced from the VD's passenger seat, her honey-blond hair falling in glinting tangles down her back, they watched from afar, hacky sacks clutched to their hearts. One glance at that Princess of Pot, that Goddess of Green, could undo, like, multimillion-dollar antidrug campaigns.

"Platinum Lexus convertible!" Taryn squawked, spewing a healthy sip of San Pellegrino Limonata into the wind.

Crap! The Nicarettes scooped up their boba teas and Post-it-tabbed magazines and tore the hell out of Melissa Moon's space. Because, as the despotic diva informed them in *no uncertain terms* when she first agreed to let them eat there, she would not, *repeat not,* hesitate to run them over.

Per the usual, Melissa and her orbiting entourage glided into the Showroom blaring Christopher Duane (aka Seedy) Moon's latest soon-to-be-octoplatinum single. Recognize that last name? Yup, rap producer icon and hip-hop heavy hitter Seedy Moon happened to be Melissa Moon's father. The new single, "V," which he wrote in one sleepless night after the now legendary Pink Party debacle, explored the intimate details of his (now ex) fiancée Vivien Ho's betrayal. The Pink Party, for the one person in the universe *not* in the know, was *supposed* to be their engagement soiree, but the glamorous gala went all horribly awry. Seedy discovered his shady fiancée had sabotaged his daughter's brand-new business. Did he mention she was *his* daughter? And what kind of whack job gets jealous of a high schooler, anyway?

And then lies about it? Over and over?

And he'd thought she was the one.

Seedy posted "V" on his Web site, Mo_Money_Mo_Moon.com, at the crack of dawn, the very next morning.

The song was spare as spare could be: no production value, no jingle-jangle, no guest vocals by the conjured ghost of Biggie Smalls, *no nothin'*. Just a man rappin' to the beat of his own broken heart, yo. The passionate, confessional, hard-as-nails single became an overnight sensation: seven million downloads and counting. Everyone was saying it — Seedy Moon was *back* — and it was a relief, since up until then his latest tunes had bombed. After making a name for himself as the first rapper to address the built-in conflict of growing up half black, half Korean in South Central L.A., Seedy had found inner peace, cranked out a series of Buddha-inspired tracks, and fell off the charts faster than you could say "downward dog." But with "V" he'd hacked up the lotus flowers and gone back to his *roots*, taking all that old anger to a whole new level. In the already notorious final verse, Seedy ties up his duplicitous ex in her own "cheap-ass, nasty" hair extensions and tosses her into the L.A. River.

"Is. It. *True?*" Carly raised her voice, squeezing each word between the booming beats quaking from Melissa's subwoofer.

"I'm not. At liberty. To say!" Nikki replied in kind, peering along with her friends from behind a camellia hedge.

Even after pulling into her spot, Melissa left the motor running and the single blaring, ensuring she and her air-freaking posse would croon every last word. Her best friend, Deena Yazdi, who fancied herself the next Mariah, fluttered her kohl-lined eyes shut, plugged one ear with a bright polished acrylic talon, and waved her free, long-fingered hand into the air. Thankfully, what Deena's voice lacked in all-things-tone, Melissa's megarack made up for in rhythm (it bounced in perfect time).

Okay, noted Nikki, polishing off her boba with a mighty slurp. *All members of Poseur accounted for* — she frowned — *except one*. Standing on her tiptoes, she scanned the now car-dominated parking lot for the missing member in question. Shouldn't she be playing third wheel to Jake and Charlotte by now? Or texting her best friend Amelia from the confines of her half-dead Volvo sedan? Or (at the very least) hiding in a bathroom stall, bemoaning the perpetually pathetic state of her very existence?

Where *was* Janie Farrish, anyway?

The Girl: Janie Farrish
The Getup: Gray American Apparel racer-back tank, black BDG skinny jeans, red high-top Converse All Stars, thirty or so black gummy bracelets, and underwear fit for a pinup (so to speak)

In eighth grade, Janie decided to practice kissing, and so (actual boys *not* being an option) started with an apricot (according to Farrah Frick, apricot skin and human lips feel *way* similar). The trouble was, after macking the orange fuzzies for say, twenty minutes, Janie ended up eating it, which made her feel kind of soulless and creepy. Like, if she wasn't careful, she might train herself into becoming the human version of a praying mantis. To stave off her guilt, she dug the moist pit out of the trash and apologized, stopping halfway through, of course, because honestly — she was apologizing to a piece of fruit. Any more of this and they'd be in a full-on relationship, which was seriously so weird they haven't even done it in Japan.

She decided to break up with apricots and graduate to something healthier . . . like her hand. Her inner elbow. She even tried her knee, pinching the skin so it resembled a protruding tongue. If tongues were riddled with shaving nicks, that is. And tasted like Skintimate.

Okay, so that didn't work either.

She moved on to the mirror — at least she'd understand the sensation of another face deliberately approaching hers, even if that face happened to be her own. Afterward, she stepped back to discover the glass mottled with drool-smeared, gaping mouth-prints. Janie pulsed with something like panic. *Did people seriously do this to each other's faces?* With a wad of paper towel and Windex, she urgently wiped them away, ignoring the mirror's plaintive squeaks. *Like, willingly?* she thought. *Like, on a daily basis?* It seemed impossible.

And yet.

She rejected physical engagement in favor of drier research. She compiled lists of how-to-kiss tips cobbled together from select magazines, slo-mo'd movies, overheard bathroom gossip, and Google. Then, just as she began to feel prepared, Amelia returned from visiting her aunt in Texas and proudly reported *she'd been kissed.* Janie swallowed her envy, even feigned happiness for her best friend, cheerfully asking what it was like. It wasn't until Amelia replied, "I dunno . . . depends on the guy," that Janie's heart grabbed her esophagus and hung itself. For the first time, Janie understood the terrible extent of her behindness. *What's the point of research?* she scolded herself. Obviously, God had a plan, and part of that plan, after dividing light from darkness, water from sky, included dividing Janie Farrish, for all eternity, from the opposite sex. (Okay, unless you count Jeremy Ujhazy, ninth-grade author of the admirably succinct "I need you," followed by "please," love notes left in her locker. But, *come on*: with his distressingly slick cherry Popsicle pout, sprouting man boobs, and evident taste for pastel pink stationery, he was more woman than *she* was.

The nice thing is, once you accept life as a predestined march through a sexless desert of meaningless despair, you can relax. Which is precisely what she'd been doing last Saturday night at the now notorious Pink Party. While everybody else mingled indoors, bubbling over with laughter and champagne, she retired to the empty pool deck, prepared to stare with resigned melancholy at the surface of the Moons' infinity pool. But then, just when she'd accepted her fate as an outsider, a wallflower, a Shakespearean clown, Evan Beverwil took a seat next to her, filling the night air with the scent of salt, sand, and sun-warmed cedar, and changed everything. After months of fleeting glances, accidental physical contact, and fumbled attempts at actual conversation, after months of wondering whether he just sort of liked her or full-on loathed her, he looked into her eyes and answered the question. He answered in a way she could not in a billion years have anticipated.

That kiss was waking up and falling asleep at the same time. That kiss was like dying, maybe. The moment their lips touched her entire being coiled into a tiny, tight ball and levitated — just a quaking planet where her face used to be. Her body ceased to exist, and then he'd touch her, conjuring it back in bursts. He'd touch her shoulder; it throbbed back to life. He'd lift his hand, and it drifted away, fading like a firework. Not that she'd notice; the next touch always eclipsed the last. Her cheek, her chin, her waist, her hip: one by one they'd explode, hot, bright, shimmering — and all the while there was that kiss, returning her to nothingness, the velvety black abyss without which she'd have never known the shivery intensity of all that light.

Let's just say the apricot did not prepare her for that.

It turned out kissing wasn't something you could research or practice, but something you had to do, like diving into the deep end to learn how to swim. Except, of course, when it came to swimming, her brother had to push her (she still hadn't forgiven him). With Evan, she hadn't needed convincing; she'd been incredibly nervous, yes. But she'd also been ready. Which is why — how else could she explain it? — the kiss had been so spectacular. At least *she* thought so. And if she thought so, he'd have to, too, right? Something so intense couldn't possibly be one-sided.

Could it?

She replayed the moment in her mind until, like a photograph passed between too many hands, it began to yellow and fall apart. By the time Sunday night rolled around she was in a state of jittery panic. What *had* happened exactly? I mean, she knew what had happened, but what made her think it had been so meaningful? After all, Evan could have just kissed her because he was drunk, or because he felt bad for her, or because, you know, it was *something to do*. It's not like kissing was a big deal for him, right? He was a *senior*. Oh, and how about how they'd parted ways? Little did they know, but as they'd kissed, a scene of epic chaos was underway indoors. Finally, the shattering sound of glass diverted their attention. Before they knew it, they were surrounded: a flood of guests streamed onto the deck, pushing one another out of the way, some of them screaming, some of them laughing. Janie and Evan leaped to their feet and fled, only to be intercepted by Charlotte and Jake. And that's when it happened.

They'd dropped hands.

It seemed perfectly natural at the time. After all, Charlotte was his *sister* — his incredibly domineering, terrifyingly popular sister — not to mention Janie's former tormentor turned colleague turned friend. Well, sort of. Charlotte wasn't exactly an *equal*. Theirs was a friendship based on power. As in Charlotte had it. Janie was beta to her alpha, squire to her queen, lowly, hunchbacked assistant to her sorceress. Was it any wonder she'd dropped Evan's hand before Charlotte noticed? He was her brother, after all — her *older* brother; holding his hand (not to mention kissing him for what must have been a full minute) was a major transgression, and not because it put her and Charlotte on equal footing. Far worse.

It made her the most powerful girl at school.

Of course, now that she'd had some time to think about it, the action wasn't so clear. She hadn't exactly had to *wrench* herself free from Evan's grip. Quite the opposite. He'd dropped her hand as much as she'd dropped his — if not *more* so — and not for the same reason, she was pretty sure. Evan didn't curtail his needs in respect to his sister's feelings — or anyone else's, for that matter. If he dropped her hand, he did so because he *wanted* to. *Don't read into this,* she ordered herself. *It's just something that happened. It doesn't have to* mean *anything.*

Except that maybe he was embarrassed of her?

By Monday morning, she'd gone completely, irrevocably bonkers. So bonkers, in fact, that when they finally crossed paths in the Showroom, and his beach glass–blue eyes settled on hers, and their gazes twisted together and locked, and he melted into a smile, and he seemed happy to see her, she was so overcome with relief that when at last he said, "Hey," she could only sigh, "Fine," but it was okay, because they both just laughed, and she glimpsed his perfect teeth, and his large, square hand in his beach-tousled hair, and then the bell began to ring, and the sun behind the trees glittered like confetti, and it filled her to the brim, like she'd just won something big, something grand, and then the bell abruptly stopped, and the air around her hummed, and he gently kicked her ankle as shyly she shook her head, grinned at the ground, and croaked, "I should probably go."

She positively floated to class; she sailed through the door, tethered herself to a chair, reeled herself into the seat, and chained herself into place. How else could she explain it? This absurd ability to *sit down*, to follow the mundane rules of gravity. In any event, she was grounded. Until her phone beeped, and the sound was a needle-size arrow of pure delight, and his text said, "God, I like looking at you," and she floated into the air again, bumping lightly along the ceiling, cell phone in hand, her thumbs almost pulsing as quickly she wrote back, "I know." Meaning, of course, she liked looking at him, too — but what if he thought she was being egotistical? She thought she should clarify, except then Ms. Bhattacharia rumbled into the room, forcing her to shut off her phone, and then, just as it powered down, *it beeped again*, and the beep echoed in her mind, again and again, like a machine that measures heart rate, until she couldn't take it anymore and excused herself to the bathroom, and it was there — with the morning light sifting through the beveled bathroom window, and three seventh-graders chattering loudly at the sinks — that she finally read his reply.

I need to see you again.

And then.

Projection room? Lunch?

At last, the bliss petered out; she plummeted out of the air and crashed to the ground. Because "Projection room?

Lunch?" really meant "Dark and empty room? Lunch?" which really meant *I will touch your boobs at lunch*. After all, lunch lasted a full *forty-five minutes*, and she couldn't depend on a celebrity-studded stampede to interrupt them. Not this time. Which wasn't to say she was against the idea of going further per se. Quite the opposite. She was pro progress. It was her *body* that was all anti. Seriously, she'd seen fifth-graders more developed than she was. And the upshot of it all was she didn't even have the nerve to change in front of other *girls* (she'd worked out a pretty awesome maneuver where she almost, like, *birthed* her sports bra through the armhole of her t-shirt), and now Evan Beverwil, whose abject, surf-god gorgeousness replaced Victoria Falls as the seventh wonder of the world, was going to slide his warm, beach-weathered hands beneath her ribbed, threadbare gray tank, and . . . what?

Mistake her for his surfboard?

And, if that wasn't bad enough, she happened to be wearing her bleach-eaten, held-together-with-a-safety-pin bra from the Gap. Seriously, the one day it mattered, she'd chosen the underwear equivalent of a lint trap? Evan was probably used to dating girls who wore couture lingerie, like, *every day*. Girls who bought panties at the rate Janie bought gum. Girls who had their bras professionally laundered in, like, baby shampoo, lavender water, and the tears of newborn pandas.

By the time the lunch bell rang, she'd settled on one of four inane speeches she had swirling in her head. "Hey," she'd begin, perhaps sheepishly biting her lip. "Look, I wanted to say hi, but actually, I can't stay. I have this, like, doctor's appointment. Yeah, my mom's picking me up. Oh, no, no, you don't have to walk me there. Seriously, my mom's, like, super weird about me walking to the car with, like, other people. Yeah, I don't know why. I should probably ask her one of these days. Okay, well . . . see you around!"

After that, she'd just hide in the bathroom for an hour. And yeah, it was a lame-ass move, but what was she supposed to do? Seal off her chest with police tape? She smiled to herself, quickening her pace. *A deconstructed pageant dress with a yellow DO NOT CROSS sash could look kind of awesome, actually.* She'd just have to pick up her sketchbook on the way to the bathroom. *Of course,* she exhaled, stopping in her tracks. *First things first.*

She opened the projection room door.

Heat bloomed across her face as he looked up and stepped toward her, reaching around her shoulders to shut the door. She sucked in her breath, knocking into a rickety fold-out table. A stack of shiny purple programs from last year's production of *Godspell* spilled to the ground and fanned across the floor. The door clicked. It was dark. The programs slithered under her feet as she creaked across the small room and perched on the sagging arm of an old club chair, sinking her palms into the worn leather, frowning at the floor. She refused to look up, not even when he put his hands on her knees, sliding them up her thighs, his thumbs following the inseam of her jeans; not even when he gripped her hips and gently urged her closer, his t-shirt sagging forward like a sail, his sweet breath in her hair. She felt weirdly furious with him, for making her feel so much, for making her want to both run and stay exactly where she was. "Hey," she cleared her throat, dimly remembering something she was meant to say. *Oh, right.* She relaxed as the words came flooding back. *The speech.* She looked up, boldly met his eyes, and repeated herself with authority. *"Hey."*

And then her arms flew around his neck, and she pulled him toward her mouth, because it wasn't a choice, because she *had* to, because blood thundered through her like a river, and each kiss was a rock, a small, jutting island.

Each kiss was a safe place to land.

spazz
hands

interlocking
G-print Carré
silk scarf

Stella McCartney
for Adidas
hoodie

Valentino Red
Pleat-front Pants

Elizabeth & James
Snake-Embossed Detail
Booties

The Girl: Melissa Moon
The Getup: White bedazzled bandanna, white Dereon Peek-a-Boo skinny jeans, white wife beater, strappy platinum Giuseppe Zanotti jeweled heels, manicure in Chanel's "Paparazzi," obvi

"*Très gentille* of you to show up, darling," Charlotte cooed as Petra traipsed into the weekly Poseur meeting, saluting her colleagues with a sloshing bottle of Kombucha tea.

"I know, right?" she replied, chucking her ratty hemp hobo onto the carpet and sprawling out beside it. She was wearing vintage jean overall cutoffs with a black Speedo racer bikini top underneath an oversize green-checked flannel, and slouchy knit boots. The ensemble was decidedly Ugg, but with her tumultuous golden mane and wide-set tea-green eyes, both shining with Visine and imperceptibly bloodshot, Petra could have made a garbage bag — sorry, an ecoconscious biodegradable *compost* bag — look like Oscar (the Grouch) de la Renta. For real, y'all.

She put the *reek* in *très chic*.

Melissa was not impressed. "I was just checkin' the agenda for today's meeting?" she announced blithely, and flapped open her white-glitter binder like someone gutting a fish. "And nowhere does it say, 'arrive late, smelling like a marijuana joint.'" She arched a ferociously gelled eyebrow at the offending hippie. "You get me?"

"I *think* so." Petra repressed a smile. Who the hell said *marijuana joint*? Could she seriously be more uptight? "But, um, I'm not really hip to your lingo."

From her station at the teacher's desk, the demanding diva's head-to-toe white ensemble complemented her glaring, white-hot rage. With her white linen pleat-pants, body-skimming wife beater, light-reflecting running jacket, and interlocking G-print carré scarf, Melissa's look was pure JLo — back in the good ol' Diddy days, of course. Melissa hardly counted Jennifer Lopez's "regular girl" Bennifer phase (not to mention her current "dead-in-the-eyes, Marc Anthony–keeps-my-soul-in-jelly-jar" phase) as fashion inspiration. "Regular" was just another word for "boring," which she was anything but. From her swinging, diamond dollar-sign necklace to her sickly high stiletto heels, Melissa could take the blah out of Blahnik.

"How's this for lingo?" Charlotte chirped from her perch on the sunny windowsill, extended her long leg to point the toe of her fuchsia suede Delman ballerina flat and addressed Petra. "If you're so much as a *minute* late to the *Nylon* shoot?" The shoe slipped from her heel, dropping like a jaw. "We stuff you into a hacky sack and feed you to the narcs."

"Okay." Petra laughed, raising her ink-stained hands in surrender. "Not to point out the obvious here? But *I* am not the last one here."

And then, as if on cue, Janie rushed through the open

door, cheeks flushed and light brown hair askew. Melissa and Charlotte shared a glance. It was totally out of character for Janie to be late. That said: Petra had a point.

"Where were you?" Melissa puffed up, fully prepared to unleash her wrath.

"Um . . ." Janie finger-combed her hair and commenced digging through her bag, as if somewhere within its chaotic depths she'd unearth an answer. Sadly, in the course of kissing Evan, her brain had died, and as coming up with good excuses was a completely brain-based activity, she was pretty much screwed. Maybe she should just tell them the truth? She looked up from her bag, catching Charlotte's cool, unreadable glance. Exactly when was the right time to tell Winston's resident ice queen you'd just spent all of lunch in a small, criminally unlit space with her totally out-of-bounds older brother? When do you tell Poseur's seamstress her brother had clutched her proverbial DO NOT CROSS sash and ripped it apart at the seams? When do you tell her you were late because you couldn't kiss him good-bye without starting the whole damn cycle over again? She cleared her throat.

"I . . ."

No. She couldn't do it. She *wouldn't*. Even that word, which was barely a word — that *letter* — which constituted exactly one-twelfth the weight of her full confession — *I was with Evan* — had proved too treacherous. For the second time that day, she recalled the Pink Party, the flustered way she'd flung off Evan's hand, her instinct (and possibly his?) to keep things private. On a gut level, she just knew:

Charlotte would have Janie's kiss-happy head on a stick.

"Omigod, *qu'est-ce que c'est* is it?" The endlessly curious Francophile tilted forward, and the corner of her beautiful and vicious mouth twitched with bemusement. From her position on the floor, a wide-eyed Petra quietly and painstakingly unwrapped a cherry-flavored Ricola, loath to break the suspense.

"I . . ."

Melissa could not be more bored. "Just sit down," she groaned, rescuing her discombobulated coworker with a startlingly loud rap of her silver Tiffany hammer. Janie wobblingly exhaled like a discharged prisoner. *Unbelievable*, she thought, obediently taking her seat. On any other day, she'd have been ruthlessly questioned (as Nikki Pellegrini could testify: interrogation was Melissa's forte), but today, on the *one* day it would have led to some serious drama, she'd been pardoned. *Seriously, what was going on?*

What was going on was this: for some endlessly mysterious reason, Janie's life had been, like, *not* sucking. In addition to the miraculous development of a love life, Poseur, the upstart fashion label for which she was one-fourth responsible, was actually taking off. Ted Pelligan, the eccentric yet omnipotent fashion luminary, was head-over-Hermès in lust with Poseur's premier designer handbag, the Trick-or-Treater. "It's heaven on a handle!" he'd assured them over Skype, while Daphne, his scowling Vietnamese manicurist, tugged his small hand and repeatedly squawked, *"Re-lax-uh!"*

"Shangri-la with a shoulder strap!"

"RE-LAX-UH!!!"

Come Thursday, Janie and her colleagues' "guardians" (to think they used to be parents!) would congregate in Mr. Pelligan's vast and polished office and sign on the dotted line, granting Pelligan Enterprises exclusive rights to produce *one thousand* Trick-or-Treaters for the small fee of (wait for it) $15,000. *To each of them.*

They were millionaires!

And then, just when she thought things could not get more awesome, the universe, like a drunk-on-the-job car salesman, went ahead and sweetened the deal. *With a freaking* Nylon *shoot.* The super-hot glossy advised them to "just, you know, come dressed like you normally dress," which everyone knew meant "dress better than you've ever dressed in your entire life." And while only last week Janie would have had to reduce herself to borrowing one of Charlotte's mother's designer castoffs, or worse, do battle with the homeless at Jet Rag's infamous Dollar Sale, today getting dressed was easy as pie. Why? Because today *she'd got her slice.*

She decided to set her budget at one thousand, which, okay, *sounds* like a lot, but Winston girls shell out that kind of cash *all the time*. Plus, she'd *earned* it. Plus, she was actually being super frugal with her choices. *Par exemple:* instead of the $620 "cleavage guarantee" La Perla set she really wanted, she settled for the *much* more reasonable $145 Cosabella. See? She'd just saved $475 that could be donated to a philanthropic cause.

Like shoes.

"*Girl*," Melissa huffed, startling the vaguely smiling Valley girl from her daydream. "Are you going to pay attention? Or do I need to send you a Mother McMuffin *bill* . . . ?"

"Sorry," she blushed, stooping to retrieve her pencil, which — in what may have been an attempt to escape the mounting tension — had rolled off the desk and dramatically thwacked the floor.

"As I was saying." The Director of Public Relations arched a reproving eyebrow and slowly turned, flicking on her latest PowerPoint presentation. In an instant, three words marched across the screen, POSEUR'S TOP THREATS, subjecting her colleagues to mild trepidation. Somehow, Melissa's handwriting succeeded in being both bubbly and menacing, like a Murakami cartoon or Willy Wonka's man-dicing "fizzy drink" machine. Of course, Melissa was impervious to its effects; she clicked a tiny gray remote with her acrylic-armored thumb, an absolute pillar of badass.

"Oona Berlin," she gravely announced as a photograph snapped on the screen. A raven-haired Zooey Deschanel–type looked up from a table of fabric swatches, her slightly parted cherry lips and big blue eyes conspiring to project the essence of indie innocence. "Clothing designer from New York. Nineteen years old." Melissa narrowed her eyes until they sparked.

Click.

Oona and her whimsical face were taken over by an exuberant boy wearing red footy-pajamas and what looked like a deconstructed Easter bonnet. He bounded joyously through an open field. "Algernon Getty," the charm-immune diva pronounced. "Seventeen years old. A self-described 'fab hatter' from New Orleans, Louisiana."

She zoomed up to his grinning, gleeful face. *Click.*

A bespectacled, race-and-gender-neutral baby face with bejeweled skull rings affixed to the five points of his or her bright green Mohawk glared menacingly at the screen.

"Yumi Mendez," Melissa explained. "Jewelry designer from Berkeley, California. Thirteen years old."

The projector lingered on Yumi for another two seconds and then clicked to black. Melissa lowered the remote to the desk and faced her colleagues, clasping her hands into a steeple under her chin. "Twenty designers chosen to appear in the March issue, but only *one*" — she paused for dramatic effect — "wins the cover. The question is, Will it be us? Or one of these three jokers?"

"I guess we'll find out!" brightly chirped Janie, eager to make up for her earlier lack of participation.

"No." Melissa slapped the desk. "We will *not* 'find out,' okay? Because finding out gives *them* the power. *They* need to find out from *us*, ya hear? The winner," she exhaled, "is Poseur."

"So . . ." Charlotte smirked. "Do we text them?"

"Close!" Melissa clapped her hands together and pranced toward the board, missing Charlotte's sarcasm by a mile. "Okay now." She grinned, picked up a piece of pale pink chalk, and proceeded to scrawl *Dear Nylon* in her trademark terrifying cursive. "I need y'all to channel your inner Omarosas and help me draft the *most* persuasive letter of all—"

Before she could say *time*, the chalk snapped in half. "Shoot," she muttered, scowling at the floor and regarding the two pieces with disgust. Was she really supposed to draft what would go down in history as her *most powerful missive to date* with this pathetic weakling, this *cripple*? Ha! Not a chance. With a disdainful brush of her hands, she bent toward the teacher's desk, pulled open a drawer, and . . .

Let out a loud and bloodcurdling scream.

"What the hell, Melissa!" Petra flinched against the recycling bin and covered her ears with her ink-stained hands. But the dismayed diva could only point into the open drawer, covering her mouth with her hand. After a shared glance, the three remaining girls abandoned their respective posts and ventured slowly toward the desk. Charlotte saw it first, and finding no French words worthy, resorted instead to an English classic:

"Ew."

Nesting on top of a lumpy pillow and pill-ridden blanket, a frayed yellow toothbrush, dented travel-size toothpaste, purple plastic hairbrush, and can of Suave hairspray jumbled together like bugs under a rock. A pineapple-shaped clip-on earring gleamed.

"Gold plated." Melissa shuddered, slamming the drawer shut.

"Double ew." Charlotte waved her hands in revulsion, flouncing from the scene. "Is someone, like, *living* here?"

"Ch'ello Poh-czars!" A Russian accent floated from down the hall. A second later Miss Paletsky, their sickly sweet if criminally unfashionable twenty-eight-year-old Special Studies adviser, popped her face into the room, her feathery bangs lacquered into a nightmarish halo around her otherwise dreamy heart-shaped face. Thanks to a pair of overstuffed shoulder pads, her navy knit sweater hung from her shoulders like a large FOR RENT sign, its ugliness challenged only by the matching navy L'eggs under her pleated beige skort. *Where do people even* find *skorts in this day and age?* wondered Melissa, almost in awe.

"Ch'ow *are* you?" Miss Paletsky cheerfully asked. Pushing

an unpolished finger under the left lens of her octagon-shaped glasses, she carefully picked away some sleep.

"You would not believe it, Miss P," Melissa began, and gestured to the desk, fully prepared to debrief their loyal mentor. "We think . . ."

"We're fine!" Petra stepped in front of Melissa and grinned, maniacally nodding her head. "We think we're just fine. Thank you."

Melissa fluttered her eyelashes, appalled. "Excuse me?"

"Well, weren't we all just saying how the four of us thought we'd *never* be able to work together? You know, because we were all just so, ha! You know?"

Understandably, this inanity was met with a collective befuddled glance.

"But *now*," she continued, and linked her teacher's arm, gently urging her toward the door, "we are all just so totally, totally tight, and we have *you* to thank for it, Miss Paletsky, because without you we would have never teamed up for a Special Studies class and formed this totally rockin' fashion line. I mean, seriously? We should, like, send you a fruit basket, or something."

It was the most anybody present had heard Petra speak at one given time. Miss Paletsky seemed particularly moved, her brown eyes sparkling in gratitude behind her LensCrafters. *My ch'eart is so full!* She nodded once, swallowed back tears, and bowed her exit. Petra shut the dark green door and leaned against it, sighing a sigh of unfathomable relief.

"So," Melissa stepped in front of her, folded her oyster white running jacket—clad arms, and nodded with new understanding. "It's *you*."

"Come on, Pet . . . *squatting?*" Charlotte gripped the windowsill and shook her head in disbelief. "I mean, I *realize* you're dating someone in a band now, but aren't you taking this whole punk thing a little far?"

Janie wandered back to her chair, chewing her thumbnail. She hated to think it, but she had to agree.

"Um, *I'm* sorry." Petra sprung off the door, gaping at their ignorance. "But did you guys *not* notice something off about Miss Paletsky's outfit?"

Melissa scoffed. "Did I *not* notice the sky was blue?"

"She was missing an *earring*," Petra rejoined. Charlotte sighed, fluttering her chlorine eyes to the ceiling.

"Get to the *point*, Nancy Drew."

Petra stepped toward her, and lowered her voice. "As in a *gold-plated pineapple earring?*"

Charlotte and Melissa locked eyes.

"Miss Paletsky?" Janie squeaked, glancing between them in horror. "Miss Paletsky's the squatter?

It made perfect sense, actually. Miss Paletsky couldn't still be shacking up with her now ex-fiancé, especially not after the major drams that went down. See, Seedy and *his* now ex-fiancée, Vivien Ho, had hired the diminutive

Russian to play piano at their engagement party, and —
assuming Seedy and Vivien exemplified true love (because
who could not be in love with Seedy Moon?) and conclud-
ing it was wrong to marry without it — she had worked
up the courage to break off her engagement. A bold move,
considering losing Yuri meant losing her chance at citizen-
ship, a convenient fact the sweat-stained owner of the Copy
& Print Store on Fairfax never let her forget, consistently
barking, "They will send you back to Russia. Like *dog*!" But
Miss Paletsky refused to care. When it came to choosing
between her nonexistent green card and her barely existent
dignity, she chose the latter, and against all inclination to be
agreeable stormed out of his Putin-infested apartment. He
could fend for himself on his toadstool leather couch, with
his Icy Hot, with his bull neck, with his Tivo'd episodes of
The View. For once, she didn't care where she was going. And
then she realized.

She had nowhere to go.

Not that Yuri let her off the hook. Convinced there was
another man, the squat vigilante infiltrated the Pink Party
with his *Bratva*, an elite band of criminals existing in Russia
since the days of the tsar, or, in Yuri's special case, a ragtag
band of petty crooks in waiter uniforms, and then — in
front of all those people; in front of Seedy! — accused his
would-be bride of "lying with pigs." Needless to say, Seedy,
who had a posse of his own, leaped to her rescue, and as

that *particular* party was bullet-free, the two gangs had no choice. Before the inevitable loser could belt out "Food fight!," the Pink Party had dissolved from a perfect rose-tinted confection to a Pepto-Bismol-pink-stained nightmare. Tables wheeled across the floor, cakes soared, ice sculptures exploded. But nothing moved with greater velocity than Miss Paletsky herself, who — wracked by humiliation — flew from the spectacle and escaped into the night.

"I mean . . ." Petra resumed her seat on the floor. "Where else is she supposed to stay?"

"Not with that Russian dude," Melissa declared, pushing some air between her lips.

"Doesn't she have any friends?" opined Charlotte.

"Poor Miss Paletsky!" Janie exclaimed, mutilating her thumbnail. Did she honestly have no better option than sleeping at *school*? Was she really and truly . . .

Ch'omeless?

The Girl: Amelia Hernandez
The Getup: Pink fishnet Hot Topic t-shirt with black thrift store tank underneath, black pin-striped Forever 21 pants, black and white plastic bangles from Claire's, black Doc Martens, manicure (in Wite-Out)

"Dude." Amelia Hernandez, Janie's very best friend since childhood, appeared at the top of an elegant flight of polished white marble stairs that led to Ted Pelligan's second floor, and held up an acid blue t-shirt. The word TRASH pranced across the distressed fabric in bold black caps. "Guess how much?"

"I don't know. . . ." Janie craned around a clearish pink fiberglass palm tree and squinted. Bowler hats clustered above her head like coconuts. French pop pulsed. "Fifty?"

"Three hundred and forty-nine," Amelia informed her, frowning her disapproval at the shirt. She resembled a ventriloquist addressing her badly behaved dummy. "I mean, is this a joke?"

"Nah," Janie tried on a yellow Katie Mawson porcupine hat and tilted her head, regarding herself in a silver-framed full-length mirror. "The JOKE shirt costs twice as much." Catching her friend's sickened glance, she pushed out a laugh — but her heart wasn't in it. For once, she didn't feel like making fun of the clothes at Ted Pelligan. Because for once she had $15,000 in her very near future. Which meant for once she was going to buy something.

She draped a Robert Rodriguez Black Label strapless sequin dress over a slender arm and smiled. *Good-bye mockery. Hello frockery.*

"It's like, if you took one homeless guy, plucked at random from Third Street, and put him next to some *gazillionaire*, like, outfitted in head-to-toe Ted Pelligan, do you honestly think anyone would tell the difference?" Amelia dropped the shirt like a used Kleenex and flounced downstairs. "It's like that game, European or Gay." She sidled up to the mirror and licked her finger, fixing some wayward liquid eyeliner. "The Hollywood Jackass edition."

Janie, who barely managed to nod in response, handed her selections to a striking salesgirl. "Okay." She turned to Amelia, her delicate face awash with worry. "Troubadour. What are you going to wear?"

Amelia grinned. Creatures of Habit, her super fierce neopunk band, had booked the legendary club for the first time last week. The Troubador was the stomping ground of everyone from Miles Davis to Metallica, *not to mention the last place Janis partied before she died.* Hello? Can we say major ghost points?

"I think I'll just wear the London Vampire Milkmaid Dress," Amelia confessed, referring to the badass dress Janie designed. "That dress is pure magic, man. The more I wear it, the better it gets. *Like a fine wine*," she mused, her hands pressed to her heart.

"Ha," Janie cracked, masking her pleasure. "Except you drink wine out of plastic cups."

"Yeah, well . . ." Amelia smiled distractedly. "Honestly, I can't think about what I'm going to wear. I'm too worried Paul's gonna to bail on the show to, like, bake gluten-free zucchini bread with his freak girlfriend."

"She's not a *freak*," Janie defended Petra, hiding a smile.

"*Whatever*," Amelia gaped. "Ever since she and Paul started dating? He's turned into this total, like, *hemp* seed. I told you he took out all his piercings, right? I swear, if you look closely, you can see his *real* personality, like, trickling out of the holes."

"I don't know. . . ." Janie shrugged. "Maybe *this* is his real personality. You never know. Maybe who he was before was the fake version."

"Wow." Amelia smirked, rolling her eyes. "Look who's so evolved. *I wonder why*."

Janie smiled. She knew what Amelia was getting at: as recently as last week, she'd been brutally obsessed with Paul Elliot Miller, i.e., any details about his and Petra's budding romance would have sent her into cardiac arrest. *But now?* Spying a silk tank in deep chlorine blue, she thought of Evan's eyes, fingered the delicate fabric, and sighed.

"Do you like?" She smoothed the silky blue-green fabric

over her long, thin torso.

"Meh." Amelia shrugged. She pointed out the same tank in red and black, Janie's favorite colors. "Check it out."

"Oh right." She affected a pensive expression, only briefly acknowledging the other tank before returning to the one in blue. "I just like this one for some reason. Wait while I try it on?"

"A'course," Amelia assured her, plucking a pair of pink Ed Hardy tattoo-hearted sweats off the rack. She whip-turned toward a pouty salesgirl. "Do you have these in medium?" Janie giggled, heading toward the fitting room. Amelia never left a store without trying on the most hideous thing she could find. (She called it the *Que La Chinga* Challenge.)

". . . to *kiss* her?!" a girl's voice almost yelled just as Janie entered her stall and clattered the lock. Janie stared at the partition, but the girl, no doubt sensing an intruder, lowered her voice to a hoarse whisper. *Puh-lease*, Janie rolled her eyes and shimmied out of her wife beater.

Like she cared.

"I'm sorry," the disembodied voice continued. "It's just . . . of all the girls in the world, why *her*? No, I *know*. It's just . . . was she a good kisser?"

Janie squared her shoulders and faced the mirror. *God*, she thought, fingering the safety pin in her bra strap. She could not *wait* to buy a new bra.

"Liar," the girl next door giggled, her voice gradually mounting in volume. "No, she did *not*. She did *not drool*. You are so full of . . . what?" She gasped, pealing with melodious laughter. "She kisses like a *dogfish*, what? What in the hell is a *dogfish*?"

That laugh, Janie realized, staring at the partition a second time, *sounded all too familiar*. But was it really her? If so, who was she interrogating?

"Ja-nie-kins!" Amelia's voice rose above the pulsing music, bubbling brightly into the room. "I'll show you mine if you show me yours!"

"One sec!" Janie yanked the silky green tank over her head, quickly smoothed her hair, and exited the fitting room. Amelia turned from a triple-angle outside mirror, where she'd been admiring her butt cleavage in its hideous Ed Hardy–exposed splendor, and narrowed her liquid eye-linered eyes. "Well?" her best friend inquired. "What's the verdict?"

"I don't know," Amelia admitted. Which wasn't to say she didn't think Janie looked hot. She did. But she also looked rich. And, like, *mean*. Like the popular girl in an eighties movie with better hair. "Maybe it's just a little generic," she exhaled.

"Generic?" An incredulous salesgirl looked up from a "rejects" clothes rack and abruptly ceased sifting. Her huge, star-lashed amber eyes perfectly matched her blond

Balayaged afro. "Sweetie," she sighed, and emphatically impaled her hair with a purple pick. "That tank is *not* generic, it's *versatile*. For day, you dress it down with some cute little high-waisted shorts and fun wedges. For night, you throw on a statement necklace, a shrunken blazer, and *walla*! Instant glamour."

"Totally," agreed Janie, ignoring Amelia's contorted *ew* face in favor of making mental inventory of the things she'd now need to purchase along with her "versatile" tank: *cute little high-waisted shorts, fun wedges, statement necklace, shrunken blazer. . . .*

"I have it in every color," gushed the salesgirl, "but that blue-green's definitely my favorite."

"I know, mine, too." Janie almost blushed, briefly fantasizing an imaginary friendship with this way older, way hipper woman. They'd share silky tank tops, paint each other's nails black, sashay down Melrose in bug-eyed sunglasses and, scowling at those less awesome than they. . . .

"As soon as I get my paycheck," she addressed her soon-to-be BFF, "I'm so coming back and buying it."

"You don't have a platinum Pellicard?" The salesgirl wrinkled her gleaming brow in concern.

"Oh." Janie's face fell, loath to disappoint her new muse so soon.

"Don't worry," she beamed, fluttering her light, cool fingers to Janie's bare shoulder, "I can hook you up right now. Seriously, it's super easy to sign up, *and* you get a free gift with every thousand dollars you spend."

"Cool."

"Excuse me?" Amelia, freshly freed from her Ed Hardy grossness, clatteringly burst out of the fitting room. "Janie, you cannot be serious. A *credit* card?"

"*Pellicard*," the salesgirl corrected, ushering a hypnotized Janie out of the fitting room. Amelia watched them sail away with gaping disbelief.

Then she came to her senses.

"No, your mom will seriously kill you," she warned, catching up with them at the register. "She's probably, like, beached out on your couch, watching a *20/20* special on the dangers of credit *as we speak*."

"You guys are too cute. I love how you take care of each other," the salesgirl murmured, inputting Janie's info into the computer. Then she glanced up and smiled, amber eyes aglow. "Name?" she chirped.

"Jane, um, Farrish," Janie stammered, glancing at the gaping Amelia. "It'll be *fine*," she half assured her, half assured herself. "Relax, okay?"

But before Amelia could respond, a whirling storm of spray tan, sun-in, and in-your-face sass migrated from a Balenciaga bikini display, gathered force behind a rack of See by Chloé short-shorts, and exploded on the scene. "Zanie?" Charlotte Beverwil's next-door neighbor and aspiring Oscar presenter gasped aloud. "You disgusting, fat whore, is dat *ju?*"

Janie beamed, internalizing her somewhat rattled nerves as Don John propelled Mort, his wheelchair-bound and possibly unconscious charge (not to mention his impromptu shopping cart) toward the register. In exchange for assisting the retired and ailing Hollywood producer, Don John got to live in his pool house for free. Of course, "assistant" seemed a scandalously loose term for the flip-flopping fop's primary activity: languishing poolside whilst telling Charlotte how "fierce" she looked. But whatever. With an array of candy-colored Bermuda shorts heaped on his lap and a dreamy-soft smile on his wrinkled, pink face, Mort seemed more than content.

"Is Charlotte here?" Janie asked, glancing back to the fitting room after he and Amelia were introduced.

"Well, she is in body but not in spirit," he clucked, already absorbed in a nearby mirror and sucking in his cheeks. "Oh, Loooocccie!" he sang toward the fitting rooms. "Would you please stop this interminable conversation with that silly, silly boy? We got company."

The door to the mystery dressing room finally opened then, and Charlotte emerged in a painfully chic camel-colored Chloé suit. The expertly tailored jacket and playfully scalloped shorts exuded the perfect balance between classic beauty and flirty sex appeal. It was seriously so envy-inducing

Janie almost clutched Amelia's arm for support.

"I'll call you back," the petite brunette bombshell murmured into her iPhone, immediately laying eyes on Janie. She dropped her cell into her glossy black Chanel shopper and released an airy laugh. "Janie!"

"Hey!" Janie tossed her hair and attempted to act natural. She hated to admit it, but she was one person with Amelia, and another with Charlotte. Was she really supposed to be both at the same time? "*Quel* is up?" she chirped, before catching Amelia's horrified eye. "Ha!" she laughed thinly.

"What'd you think?" The salesgirl, who'd completed Janie's app in record time, swept away from the register and beamed.

"*Hids*," Charlotte sniffed, and stuffed a lacy wad of discarded lingerie into her outstretched hands. "Cut for a drag queen."

"I'm so sorry," she gasped, as Don John peered over her shoulder, examining the rejects with new interest.

"Hello," the pretty ice queen smiled at Amelia, magnanimously extending her hand as Don John disappeared with the salesgirl. "Charlotte Beverwil."

"Charlotte's the head seamstress for Poseur," Janie babbled inanely as they limply shook hands. "Amelia goes to LACHSA. She's in a band. Creatures of Habit, actually, you know them! They're playing Friday and you should *totally* come, I mean, obvi."

"Oh, *obvi*." Amelia eyed her friend in thinly masked disbelief.

"*Trés* cool," Charlotte oozed. "Well, great to see you two, but I have got to return this call." Fishing her iPhone from her shopper, she confided, "Don't want to be rude."

The two girls followed her tiny, ticktocking hips with their eyes as she confidently headed for the all-glass double door exit. And then, just as she'd turned to Amelia with an apologetic little sigh, the French wench's melodious voice rang brightly in her ear.

"Evan?"

The blood drained from Janie's face. Wait, so, she'd been talking to *Evan*? That *entire* time? About kissing? Wait a minute. . . .

Paranoia donkey-kicked her heart.

Did that mean *she* was Dogfish?

"Wait for me, you mangy minx!" Don John cried, sweeping Mort free of garments and wheeling him toward the exit. The salesgirl flashed Janie's freshly used platinum Pellicard and sang.

"Enjoy your top!"

The Guy: Seedy Moon
The Getup: Mourning garb: coffee-stained gray sweats,
Bugs Bunny slippers, black silk Korean flag bathrobe,
no shirt, gold chains, gold rings, ink for days

Melissa returned to her über-modern glinting glass Bel Air
estate to find her father exactly where she'd left him at
eight in the morning: holed up in his second-floor studio,
tinkering away at yet another sad and pensive, soon-to-be-
voice-modulated (his voice was terrible) song about Vivien.

This one, from what she could gather from the obses-
sively repeated chorus, was titled "Float Like a Butterfly,
Sting Like a Vee." Melissa sighed with concern. Not to say
she wasn't *super* down with Daddy dumping that bitch-
ass Botoxed barracuda like he did (she was *down* to the
can-I-kiss-it *ground*). And not to say she didn't fully support his soaring rise to worldwide chart domination (she
was the wind beneath his *bling*). But, still. Him moping
around in those raggedy-ass gray sweats day after *day*?
Subsisting on nothing but Mountain Dew, melba toast,
and misery?

Nuh-uh. Not cool.

And so, in what *some* might deem a rare burst of self-
lessness and domesticity, Melissa pitched her Juicy Couture

Cheetah Day Dreamer to the immaculate white Berber carpet and padded with purpose to their ultramodern kitchen. After the requisite blowout with Mr. Thang, their nasty, totalitarian cook, she whipped her daddy up some *personalized* macaroni and cheese. It was the best mac on the planet, which was a good thing, seeing as it was the only thing she knew how to make herself.

"Daddy!" she sang, softly clunking upstairs in her Dolce & Gabbana denim platform wedges and the hideous hippie smock Petra designed for her to wear to Poseur's launch party (she'd taken to using it as a makeshift apron). She leaned against the airtight, opaque black glass door of Seedy's studio, balancing the mac on her hip. "Daddy! Open up. I brought you a *present*."

"Is it a gun?" he inquired, a note of hope in his voice. He sounded like gravel and rusty chains.

"Um, no . . ." Melissa smiled at the door, straining with cheer. "But I'll give you a hint, okay? It starts with *m*."

"Machete?"

"Daddy," his daughter huffed, shifting the mac on her hip. "Just open the door, okay? Tray's getting heavy!"

She heard something like a shuffle, and stepped back. Seedy cracked open the door and peeked out. Melissa pressed her lips together in disapproval. Here he was — the Kimchi Killa, the Lord of the Blings, the illest hip-hop artist in *history* — and what? He looked like butt. Gone was the fun-loving sparkle in his eyes. Gone the cleanly shaved head, fragrant and gleaming with coconut oil. His eyes were now bloodshot, sunken, and dull. And as for his head, *Lord*.

Looked like he was wearing George Clooney's *face* for a *cap*.

"Delivery!" Melissa chimed, as if she could combat the foul rankness of the airless studio through sheer force of pep. She floated her simmering tray (along with the mac, she'd added an origami napkin swan, a novelty silver spoon, and a bottle of VitaminWater (Rescue flavor)) into the dark, keyboard-stuffed room. "Ta-da!"

"No!" Her father waved aside a Gruyère-scented puff of steam. "Melissa, I told you I cannot *eat*."

"I know what you told me," Melissa assured him, landing the tray on top of a high-end Yamaha amp and brushing her hands. "You can't eat. You can't sleep. You can't move. . . ." She regarded her father with steely-eyed reserve, and then — quick like a Band-Aid — threw open the velvet blackout curtains.

"Aaagh!" Seedy flinched, and attempted to combat a sunbeam with a hapkido hand strike. "The *light*."

"That's right." Melissa bobbed her eyebrows. "That light is full of the vitamin D you need for such D-related activities as bein' top *dawg*, not to mention bein' my *daddy*. So stop with the woe-is-me whining, and *bake* it till you *make* it, a'ight? *Damn*."

Plopping down on the plush white leather couch, she folded her arms, bolting her father with her very sternest, do-not-mess-with-me stare. Seedy sulked his way around the room, listless as a neglected goldfish, and then surrendered, flopping into his ergonomic seat. He stared at his synthesizer, pushing some air between his lips. "D," he murmured, poking the corresponding key. Squeezing his dark eyes shut, he poked it again, singing with pained passion: *Duck* all those kisses, they didn't mean *jack*. *Duck* you, you *ho*. I don't want you *ba-a-ack*."

"Okay, Daddy?" Melissa blurted in interruption, unable to take it anymore. "Not to be a killjoy, but that's an Eamon song."

Seedy slowly nodded, still gazing at his keyboard, and then his face crumpled. *Ho no,* thought Melissa. *Was he going to cry?*

She'd have to kick it up a notch.

"Christopher Duane *Moon!*" she screeched in perfect imitation of his late mother's terrifying Korean accent. "Stop feeling so bad or I *make* you feel so very, very bad you cry like *gye jip ae!*"

Seedy sucked in his breath, stunned, and Melissa pursed her lips, triumphant. "Look, Daddy," she continued in a gentler tone. "Whenever something bad happens, all you got to do is think, *This makes room for something good*." She leaned forward, reaching for his knee. "You remember who said that?"

The mournful rap mogul gazed at his daughter, timid. "Eckhart Tolle?"

"No, Daddy. You did."

He whispered. "I did?"

"Yeah, Daddy. And you know what else you said? *That no matter how bad things get*, there're always people much worse off. I mean, just look at Miss P, for example."

"Lena?" Seedy perked up at the sound of her name. Although he'd met Melissa's mysterious teacher for a teacher-parent conference, they'd ended up bonding a bit over music. Not that they shared similar tastes in any respect — he was hard-core into hip-hop, while she was committed to classical — but still. Then, when Vivien wanted a classical pianist for their engagement party, he invited Lena to audition. Imagine his surprise when she waltzed into their living room and performed a perfectly delicate, classical rendition of his early nineties megahit "Bi Bim Bitches." Man, it damn near blew his *mind*. After that, he found himself listening more and more to classical tracks. Yeah, like, *voluntarily*. He had to admit some of those puffy-haired white dudes were all right.

Of course, it helped that Lena made him a mix.

Wondered what she thought of his?

"That's right," Melissa eagerly continued, encouraged by her father's sudden alertness. "Miss Paletsky broke up with *her* fiancé, too, remember? But unlike you, gettin' your Phantom on in a Bel Air mansion, she's got no place." Ruefully, she shook her head. "Unless you count Room 201B."

Seedy nodded in sympathy. "You mean that new hotel on Melrose with the live white tiger in the lobby?"

"No," she groaned in despair. "It's one of the rooms at Winston. Like, she's sleeping at *school*?"

"Come on," Seedy cracked a smile, refusing to buy his daughter's dramatics. "Where'd you come up with that idea?"

"Um . . . because I found all her funky toiletries in my desk drawer while conducting the Poseur meeting today?" She gaped, daring him to refute her. "For real, Daddy. Woman is *homeless*, as in without a *home*."

Seedy frowned at the floor, slowly shaking his unkempt head. "I was homeless for a while," he admitted. "Back in eighty-four. Man, those were tough times. Real tough."

He looked around his roomful of twinklingly expensive equipment and sighed, his black eyes growing glassy. "Lissa!" He smacked the arm of his seat so suddenly his daughter jumped. "We have got to help her."

"Who?" Melissa paused. "Miss P?"

"Yes, Miss P!" Seedy leaped to his feet. "I refuse to let

that good and, and *beautiful* soul sleep in a drafty old class-room. It's not right!"

"She can come live in our second guesthouse!" blurted Melissa. The Moons' second guesthouse was not only com-pletely gorgeous, but also perfectly *untouched* — unless you count the time MTV shot that episode of *Cribs*. She clapped her hands, giddy. Not only would they be helping her out, but, you know, it might be kind of fun having her around. At times, Miss Paletsky reminded Melissa of her own mom, you know, before she got cracked-out and crazy.

"Perfect!" Seedy agreed. But then his face fell. "Except."

"No!" Melissa gasped, crumpling her face like a milk carton. "No *except*!"

"Baby, calm down." Seedy laughed, the old warmth returning to his voice. "I think Lena living here is a great idea. But, you know . . . we've got to think of a good *rea-son*."

"So, um . . ." Melissa picked a dried splatter of mac from her smock. "Having to brush her teeth in the chem lab: not a good enough reason for you?"

"Lena has too much dignity to accept charity," he explained. "If we're gonna do this, we have to make it look like it's not some kind of handout."

"Oh," Melissa nodded, finally comprehending. She and Seedy slumped into their respective seats, frowning with thought. The studio hummed. She was at a loss.

Until, for the first time in days, her father cracked a blinding megawatt smile. She looked up, hopeful.

"Pass the mac 'n' cheese," he commanded. "I've got an idea."

pretty Miu Miu high heel

The Girl: Charlotte Beverwil
The Getup: Camel-colored scalloped Chloé shorts with matching jacket, beige buffalo leather Miu Miu wedges, crème and black patent Chanel shopper

Jake and Charlotte had dinner plans Wednesday night: *platonic* dinner plans, she'd reminded him over a shared plate of shoestring fries at Kate Mantilini, earlier that day at lunch. *Whatever you say*, Jake thought, printing out a comprehensive list of froufrou French restaurants, restricting his choices to four-star Romance ratings. French ambience, plus French wine, plus French food . . . French kissing had to figure in somewhere, right? Besides, Jake knew what Charlotte liked. She *was* his ex-girlfriend, after all. He steered his ancient black Volvo 240 DL down the Beverwils' sparkling gravel drive and parked, happily drumming the wheel.

At the foot of the Beverwils' 8,000-square-foot Spanish colonial estate, his pint-sized ex informed him she was "only eating at restaurants that dealt in francs." *Right*, thought Jake, retreating to the car to scan the "payment options" tab on the list he'd printed out. Only after a mortifying phone call to JiRaffe did he discover *no* restaurant in the area accepted the currency. In fact, no restaurant in the world accepted that currency, not even in France, as it had been *completely obsolete for the last decade.*

Instead of going out to dinner, like they'd planned, Charlotte and Jake decided to just drive up the coast and park outside Moon Shadows, "to talk." They then relocated to the musty backseat of the Volvo and got to work steaming up the windows. Which was A-OK with Jake. After all, what dude in his right mind preferred the taste of duck a l'orange to the taste of Charlotte a l'optimal hotness?

She was wearing this weird thing that looked like a skirt but was actually shorts, and her legs were bare and smooth and very recently shaved, he hoped, for him. Gently, he squeezed Charlotte's smooth calf and then ran his hand all the way up to her thigh, slipping beneath the silky hem of her shorts. *And she let him.*

Until she didn't.

"Stop!" she squeaked, loud and sudden like he'd stepped on her toe.

"What?" Jake jumped back. As somebody with very (*very*) little experience in the make-out department, he was perpetually petrified of screwing up. And now, it seemed, he had. Jake ran though a series of options for what he could have done wrong. Maybe he was supposed to ask before he touched her under that skirty shorts thing? Or maybe he was not supposed to touch her under that skirty shorts thing at all? Ugh . . . he could really use a manual for this hook-up stuff. A *man*-ual. He smirked, briefly amused by his lame inner joke.

"I can't do this," Charlotte announced, a bit dramatically, in his opinion. "I need air!" She scrambled away from him, and after a failed attempt to roll down the sticky car window, popped the door open and leaped from the car. Jake watched Charlotte stomp away and plant her tiny butt on the hood of his Volvo. He followed her. That much he knew he was supposed to do, even without a man-ual.

The whispering black sea stretched out before them. In the faraway distance, the Santa Monica pier sparkled against the night sky like an old Lite-Brite toy. Jake sighed.

"What?" he asked, finally. "What'd I do now?"

"You know what you did, Jake Farrish." Charlotte looked straight forward, refusing to meet his pleading brown eyes. "You did . . . Nikki Pellegrini."

He was in shock. So, this had nothing to do with him groping her thigh after all? She was seriously still peeved at him for getting way too drunk at her hoity-toity fashion party and *accidentally* macking on that eighth-grader, Nikki Pepperoni? God, of all the dumb and totally not worth it mistakes he'd made in his life — and he could count a few — the whole Nikki fiasco took the cake. Which would be one thing if the cake had been *good*. But it wasn't! It was seriously like musty old, special-dietary-needs, *nursing* home cake.

Couldn't she *see* that by now?

"I did not 'do' her, okay?" Jake clarified, pushing himself

away from the misty-damp wooden rail. "God, I told you everything you wanted to know. Apologized . . . a *thousand* times. What more can I *do*? What do you *want*?"

Charlotte folded her arms, pouting, while Jake sighed, vigorously rubbing his face. "I'm sorry. I'm just sick of having the same conversation."

"Maybe you should have thought about that before you so eagerly sampled *Prostitutti pâté* in front of, like, everybody I have *ever* known."

"I know," Jake insisted, reaching for her arm. "*Pâté* is torture. I understand that now. So, can we please just get back together?"

"No way," she huffed, shrugging away from his touch. "Can't you see how disgustingly *desperate* I would look?"

"So this is about how you *look*?" Jake fumed, beginning to pace. "Wait," he realized, stopping in his tracks. "You already *knew* there's no restaurant that takes the French franc, right? That's why you came up with the rule! So we wouldn't be able to go out. So we wouldn't be able to, like, *be* in public!"

"Don't be ridiculous!" Charlotte tossed her hair back and set her dainty jaw.

"Oh, I'm being *ridiculous*?" He lowered his voice, pointing accusingly. "Why were you so weird on the phone today? Why'd you call me *Evan*? Huh?"

"Oh!" she tsked, dismissing him with an airy laugh. "I

just . . . I ran into Janie at Ted Pelligan's, that's all."

"I don't get it." Jake shook his head. "What does Janie have to do with this?"

"Nothing! Except . . . the whole time we were talking on the phone, I'm pretty sure she was, like, *listening* in the fitting room next to mine. I just thought if I called you Evan, then she'd wouldn't realize I wasn't talking about, you know, *what I was talking about*."

"But . . ." Jake's face collapsed in confusion. "She already *knows* about Nikki, I mean . . ."

"Yeah," Charlotte interrupted, narrowing her eyes into glittering green slits. "I *know* she knows about Nikki. *Everyone* 'knows about Nikki.' That doesn't mean I want everyone to know that I, like, still *care*."

She stomped her foot, flouncing toward the car.

"It's *humiliating*, okay?"

"Fine." Jake followed after her. "I get it. It's humiliating. And that's my fault, okay? But you have *got* to decide if it's the kind of humiliating that means we're over? Or if it's the kind of humiliating that means we can work it out."

"*I don't know*," she confessed, sounding truly miserable. At last, she grabbed his hand, blinking back tears. "I don't know."

Jake sighed, clenching and unclenching his jaw. Seriously? He couldn't go through this alone. He needed outside assistance. He needed a man-ual. He needed . . .

"Counseling."

Charlotte's delicate nostril flexed as though she'd wandered into the presence of something foul. "You're not serious."

"What?" Jake gaped, tapping his heart with two fingers. "I want to get back together, okay? And I *think* you do, too. And *yet*, instead of making out in my car, like we should be doing, we're acting like my parents outside Moon Shadows. I mean, does that make sense to you? Because it sure as hell doesn't make sense to me."

"But I don't *believe* in counseling," Charlotte reminded him, twiddling the glossy amber button on her tailored jacket. "Napoleon and Josephine didn't dissect their love on some crumbly old therapist's couch, okay? They believed in destiny. In *fate*."

"Char—" Jake smiled, cupping his slightly cracked ex-girlfriend's china cup chin in his hands. "This isn't eighteenth-century France. There are options." One hand abandoned her face and reached for the back pocket of his faded gray corduroys. "Check it out," he smiled nervously, presenting a tightly folded printout, otherwise known as his last hope, to the girl of his dreams. "Her name's Hortense Bonnaire," he explained. "She combines traditional psychotherapy with French existentialist philosophy. She's supposed to be really cool."

Charlotte took the page and scanned it timidly. In the

distance, a wave crashed.

"First session's free," he added.

"Okay," she conceded finally, with a shrug of her ballet-toned shoulders. "I guess it can't hurt."

"Great," Jake exhaled, endlessly relieved. Charlotte smiled.

Was it just her or was he totally maturing?

Jake smiled back.

Who wouldn't entrust his relationship to a chick whose last name sounded like "boner"?

Petra's Favorite Dress ☀ ☀

↑ choose your platform

The Girl: Petra Greene
The Getup: Vintage Navajo dress, scuffed beige Calypso espadrilles, dreamcatcher earrings from Venice Boardwalk, crocheted hemp hobo bag

That same crisp December night, just across town, Petra Greene and Paul Elliot Miller were strolling through the wide, tree-lined streets of Beverly Hills enjoying each other, along with some seriously chronic weed.

Since they'd first met on either side of the fence of their adjoining backyards, Petra and Paul had been virtually inseparable. Sharing joints through the ivy-entangled fence had soon given way to moonlit swims in Paul's grandparents' kidney-shaped pool, which before long turned into surreptitious whiskey sipping in Petra's little sisters' backyard playhouse, which soon enough morphed into surreptitious whiskey-fueled makeout sessions in Petra's little sisters' backyard playhouse, which soon enough turned into, well, more. . . .

They looked a little random and mismatched, but that's what Petra loved about their coupling. *The punk rocker and the flower child.* Of course, when Christina Boyd mentioned they "kinda had a Joel Madden–Nicole Richie thing going on," she'd had to put down her fried shiitake dumpling and quietly gag.

The unlikely twosome embarked on their first public outing at Seedy Moon's now infamous Pink Party. No more hiding their love in the looming black shadows of their adjacent Beverly Hills estates: they were finally *real*. "You're *real*?" Joaquin Whitman frowned over his guitar and tightened a string, barely disguising his jealousy. "You mean you're, like, official?" But no. Petra loathed that word (could anything sound more *corporate*?). *Real* was better. *Truer*. The last time she and Paul kissed — on her balcony, with moonlight sifting through the giant pine in her yard — she chanted it to herself like a blessing: *This is real, this is real, this is real, this is real. . . .*

But then *this* got weird.

Maybe it was the pot. Even seasoned stoners like Petra endured the occasional bout of marijuana-induced paranoia. Then again, maybe it *wasn't* the pot. Four days after that magical balcony night, as they strolled down one of the pristine, hedge-bordered blocks of their Beverly Hills neighborhood, taking what they jokingly referred to as "one of their nature walks," Paul noticed a dead sparrow in the gutter, his little eyes all squinched, his tiny wings wet with dew, and promptly began to *freak out*. And, not to say she wasn't pro *sensitivity* (the more people show their feelings the better), but there was something about Paul's *particular* display: it seemed a little put on. As soon as the thought nudged into her mind, however, she pushed it out, her heart skittering in panic. Had she really just suspected Paul Elliot Miller, her first love, *her partner in the real*, of being phony? She had to be wrong! And yet, as he stretched out and panted on the pavement, tears squeezing from the corners of his eyeliner-free eyes, she couldn't help but notice.

Things had changed.

Gone were the bicycle chains that had once slung seductively from his narrow hips; in their place, a macramé belt with swirly blue Fimo beads had appeared. He'd removed every last piercing — the silver hoop on his left brow, the pretty spike in his full lower lip — and had stopped dyeing his hair, the electric blue she'd fallen in love with slowly washing out, leaving his hair a murky grayish-brown that was really no color at all; a color like dishwater.

But no, Petra refused to dwell on the negative, and so she *changed her mental channel*, a trick she'd made up as a kid to keep her from obsessing over her screwed-up family. When her mom got so zonked on pills the nanny had to take over car pool; when her father bailed after dinner to "pick up a magazine," only to return hours later, rumpled and empty-handed (if he returned at all, that is); when someone kept calling the house, hanging up when Petra answered, she fluttered her tea green eyes shut, took a deep breath, and *changed the channel*. Ten years later, it still worked.

"Come on." She smiled serenely, helping him off the

ground and slinging a long arm across his shoulders. "We can go get a shoe box and bury it."

Paul exhaled a shuddering breath and quietly gulped, consoled. They walked on in silence. Sun filtered through the pines and stroked their faces. At the corner, a sleek black Bentley purred to a stop.

"You know what would be so cool?" Petra ventured as they approached a dusty peach Spanish villa with a small replica of the Statue of Liberty in the middle of the lawn. "If there was, like, an iPod you could just play, like, through your skin or something? It'd be, like, wherever you went, you'd have this theme song, you know? Like you'd be approaching this group of people and they'd just know you were coming and, like, what you were about, not 'cause they *saw* you or anything, but because they, like, *heard* you."

Paul stopped dead in his tracks, pulling Petra toward him by her slender waist. His mismatched eyes — one bluish-green, the other greenish-brown — pierced hers with intensity.

"What?" she laughed, both a little turned on and a little weirded out.

"That," Paul began, "is seriously the most genius thing I have ever heard. Petra, like, *how* did you just think of that? How the hell did you just think of that?"

"Um, I don't know." She glanced at him quizzically — was he joking? — and flushed. "I guess I just, like, thought of it."

"Seriously," he proclaimed, shaking his head. "We should go home and patent that shit, like, right now." He stared at her, his eyes slightly bloodshot (he's just stoned, Petra reminded herself), his face melting into that syrupy-lovesick expression that's so enthralling on a guy you adore and so repugnant on a guy you don't. "Petra," he marveled. "You're amazing."

"Awww," Petra replied, encouraging him to continue walking.

"A human iPod," he mused through the intermittent slap of his new Teva Bowen Stitch flip-flops. "An *iHuman* . . ."

"Speaking of music," Petra blurted, valiantly pushing through the static. "I seriously cannot wait till Friday night. I mean, *the Troubadour.* You know Janis, like, practically *died* there, right? *Oh,*" she gasped, and grabbed her boyfriend's thermal-clad arm, eyes alight. "Is it true Face-humpers might do a surprise set?"

"Wait a minute, you *heard* that?" Paul's brow wrinkled with concern. "Oh, *man.* They approached us last week, but I was, like, *no. No goddamn way.*" He frowned. "Amelia better not be going behind my back, man."

"Okay," Petra pressed two fingers to her temple and closed her eyes. "Um, I thought they were, like, your favorite band of all time?"

"Well, yeah," he admitted. "I *used* to like them. But now,

it's, like, I listen to their music and it's just so . . ." He paused to glance skyward. "*Angry*. It's, like, *why*, you know? Why put that energy into the universe? It's not helping anyone. It's not helping *me*. It's just . . . I want Creatures of Habit to be couriers of *beauty*, you know? Couriers of *peace*."

You're kind of being a courier of nausea right now, Petra thought, heat prickling along her hairline like Malibu brush fire. Okay, she was code-red wigging out, and it wasn't just the chronic. She could deal with Paul's new wardrobe — that was just superficial stuff — but denouncing the Facehumpers, a staggeringly awesome band *he turned her on to*, because they were suddenly too *angry*? He had to be joking! It was one thing for Paul to give up studded belts and chipped black nail polish. But to give up on *anger*? What about the afternoon they spent smashing her parents' wedding china in an alley? Or that night they ran screaming along the beach, hurling rocks at the moon, cursing the names of those who'd dared to cross them? Was he planning to give that up, too?

Thankfully, Petra's cataclysmic thoughts were cut short by a deep buzzing in her crocheted hemp hobo bag. "Just a sec," she told Paul, sifting through a sea of rolling papers, gum wrappers, loose beads, and dollar bills to unearth her scuffed purple Nokia. A text from Queen Moon (she'd entered her own name in Petra's cell, and Petra didn't care enough to change it):

CHECK EMAIL.

NYLON COVER NO GO.

WTF WTF WTF.

"What is it?" Paul inquired, noticing Petra's solemn face. She sighed, showing him the tragic text. "Ah, man . . ."

"I know," she agreed. Seriously? Melissa had sent *Nylon* the most persuasive e-mail of all time! "*Poor Melissa,*" she thought out loud. "She must be seriously buggin'."

"Yeah, well," Paul laughed. "That girl pretty much invented buggin', so . . ."

"*Don't be mean.*" Petra pushed his shoulder and beamed. *That he still had it in him!* She was endlessly relieved. "I know she comes off, like, *intense* or whatever. But that's what's so awesome about her. She's passionate."

"Well," Paul responded in a gravelly voice, a promisingly naughty smile creeping across his gorgeous face. He gripped her by the shoulders, pushed her up against somebody's bougainvillea-covered four-car garage, locking her into his mismatched gaze. "I guess I can identify."

She smiled, a jolt of electricity surging through her entire body. "You can?" she almost whispered, lacing her voice with sweetness.

He pressed his long and perfect body against hers, answering the way she hoped he would. More and more relief wrapped her in its warm embrace, cocooning her from fear. His kiss was deep, exhilarating, and pure.

His kiss was real.

To my wretched and most wrong'd wrens:

It is with shock in my heart and outrage in my loins that I write to you of NYLON'S regrettable decision.

In a masterstroke of sartorial injustice, this *GAG-azine* has selected *Schizo Montana* to grace the cover of their *20 Under 20* issue.

Before this fateful day, I'd remained blissfully unaware of *Schizo Montana* and their nefarious misdoings. Fortunately, Mr. Gideon Peck, my faithful and formidable assistant, is a highly accomplished computer operator. Employing something called "Goggle," he revealed to me the following exclusive facts:

1. When not colluding with the NYLON heretics, *Schizo Montana* "designs and manufactures t-shirts."
2. A t-shirt is a lightweight pullover shirt, close fitting, with a round neckline and short sleeves.

Still, my cheated chickens, my unhappiest hatch-lings, *we must not despair.* Before the kingdom, Valentino was bankrupt. Before she was a leg-end, Chanel was a steel welder. True stars are not always immediately recognized, my lovelies. And the greatest stars burn brighter with time.

To standing on the shoulder pads of giants!

Teddy

The Girl: Miss Paletsky
The Getup: What difference does it make anymore?

The snow fell from the black night sky, drifting like ash, blanketing the landscape in eerie quiet. Miss Paletsky blinked as the slushy granules stung her eyes. Icy gusts of wind penetrated her thin wool coat and gnawed her bones like a dog, bored and deadly. She was on her back, looking up, and gripping a cold metal rail; her fingers stuck like tongues. Where *was* she?

As if to answer, the hard plank under her spine began to gently vibrate, and the iron rail to hum. In the faraway distance, there was a long and ghostly wail. *A train*, she realized, and then the whole world began to quake. Planks clattered like broken rattles. The iron rail screamed. Miss Paletsky struggled to move, but she couldn't budge.

With horror, Miss Paletsky saw the train burst through the gray wall of drifting snow and come barreling toward her, blinding her with its light. Black clouds churned from its tall black smokestack.

The conductor angled his face out of the window.

Ch'elp! Miss Paletsky attempted to scream, but only produced the tiniest of squeaks, like a mouse flung by its tail through an open kitchen window. The conductor's thick ham hock of an arm waved wildly through the smoke. *He sees me!* Miss Paletsky realized, praying for a squeal of brakes, the telltale shudder of iron and steel. She focused on the gesticulating arm until, with dizzying clarity, a certain physical detail jumped out at her, obliterating all comfort.

She recognized that yellow armpit stain. . . .

"Life is not Cinderella!" he cried as the train screamed in panic, rumbling closer and closer. *Yuri!* Miss Paletsky realized, a hot tear sliding from her eye.

Her life was officially kaput.

But then, just as she'd made her peace with fate, a dark, cloaked figure swooped toward her and snatched her high into the air. She landed with a thud, all the breath leaving her body, and then, in the same moment she thought that she was dead, discovered herself thrown across a horse's back. With a quavering sigh, she surrendered to the roiling, muscular surface, breathing deep the earthy smell of animal sweat. The thundering sound of hooves met her ears like a lullaby.

Still, was she was safe? After all, she was not alone. A mysterious man sat mere inches away, his strong, straight torso like a pillar. The back of his head offered her little clue: was he friend or foe? Savior or jailor? Here she was, tossed across his horse like so much cargo; had her situation gotten worse?

Just then, a snowflake grazed her cheek, but instead of a feathery chill, it transferred actual warmth into her flesh.

Timidly, she lifted her head, looking around. They were in a beautiful orchard. The snowflake wasn't a snowflake after all, but a cherry blossom. They were everywhere, drifting from branches, pirouetting in the sun, and thickly carpeting the ground.

It was spring.

Miss Paletsky relaxed, and her heart slowed to match the horse's easy, peaceful pace. She glanced again at the man and trusted him, allowing herself to admire his perfect posture, his tall fur hat, his polished black boots. Then, her curiosity got the better of her. Harnessing her every ounce of courage, she tapped the mysterious horseman's broad and powerful shoulder.

He began to turn around—

Tap, tap, tap, tap, tap . . .

She gasped awake and sprang up from her green velvet office couch, tumbling her collection of tiny decorative pillows to the floor. "One moment!" she replied, suppressing her panic.

How long had they been knocking?

What time was it?

Had school started already?

Miss Paletsky gathered her shabby possessions, rushed to her desk, and squished her thin blanket and lumpy pillow into the drawer she'd used to store that day's change of clothes: teal stirrup leggings, white crocheted cardigan, and a camisole in pink zebra print. *Chert poberi!* She didn't want to open the door wearing the same navy sweater and beige skort she'd worn the day before. Did she have time to change?

Tap tap tap! Tap tap tap!

With a small grunt of exertion, she threw on a lime green blazer, and pulled her hair back into a fresh crushed velvet scrunchie. She reached for a half-empty travel-size can of Suave hair spray, twisted the cap off with a quiet pop, and sprayed a foggy cloud in the vague vicinity of her crunchy chestnut hair and, unthinkingly, her armpits. She took a deep breath and scurried to the door. And then, as she wrenched it open, hair spray stung her nostrils. She inhaled sharply.

And sneezed like a greedy truffle-seeking pig.

"Bless you."

Melissa Moon's impossibly gorgeous father, i.e., the last person in the world she wanted to bless her in her horrifically disheveled state, beamed down at her. Due to a morning hip-hop Vinyasa class and general Seedy Moonness, the music mogul exuded strength, compassion, and serenity. In his presence, Miss Paletsky felt like something planted next to a major four-lane highway, one of those sad, old bushes choked by toilet paper and tinsel.

"Good morning, Lena," he intoned, his voice as rich and buttery as a meat-filled piroshki on Sunday morning. "How are you?"

Miss Paletsky had not seen him since the tragic Pink Party, and, well — wow. For somebody who'd lost his fiancée just days before, he looked pretty put together. *Unlike me*, she scolded herself, *who looks like case of baskets*, Seedy was perfectly contained by his plush gray cashmere tracksuit and crisp white wife beater. A collection of gold necklaces and flashy medallions glittered on his broad chest.

But nothing compared to the brightness of his smile.

"I am so ch'appy to *see* you, Mr. Moon!" Miss Paletsky exclaimed, discreetly shelving her hair spray behind a book. "I . . . I ch'ave to say I am *so sorry* about what ch'appened with me and Yuri at your party. I wanted to call you, but—"

"You have *nothing* to apologize for," Seedy assured her, waving aside her embarrassment. "If anything, I should thank you. I mean . . . your music was the only thing *about* that party that wasn't toe-up. And you and Yuri didn't ruin my party. Me and Vee ruined my party."

Miss Paletsky nodded, fighting a lump in her throat. It was difficult to hear them paired off that way, even in past tense. "You and Yuri." "Me and Vee." The former mortified her beyond measure (what did he think of her? Associated with a man like that?), and the latter shattered her heart.

"That guy seemed pretty crazy, though," Seedy observed, interpreting her cowed silence as fear. "Has he been leaving you alone?"

"Dah, yes," Miss Paletsky replied, waving off his concern. "I am perfectly safe." Why was he here? she wondered. Perhaps he wanted her to pay for the damage Yuri caused? She could never afford it, even if, putting sentiment aside, she forced herself to sell the contents of the Pink Party gift bag on Amazon. She liked the pink iPod nano, of course, which came loaded with songs by a Fergie. She liked the Fergie.

But most of all she liked that *he* (indirectly, yes, but still!) had given these things to *her*.

"So, Lena, I know you're real busy with school and all, but I have a business proposition for you," Seedy began. Miss Paletsky was confused, so she smiled dumbly, revealing her overlapping eyetooth.

"How would you feel about teaching Melissa to play the piano? Ever since you came over and played for us, the girl will not stop begging me for lessons, so I thought, hey! Who better to teach her the ropes than the woman who inspired her, right?" His perfect teeth were white as snow.

"Melissa?" Miss Paletsky asked. "She is interested in classical music?"

"Yeah, I know what you're thinking," Seedy chuckled. "I

barely believed it myself! But what can I say, Lena? You've converted us."

"Thank you," Miss Paletsky replied, once she remembered how to speak. God, it was hot in here. Must be the blazer. . . .

"So, there's only one catch," Seedy began, preparing to floss his acting chops. (He hadn't used them since he was impaled on a meat hook in the straight-to-DVD film *Soju Slayer* back in 2004, but he knew he still had it.) "I really want to get Melissa a teacher who can live on the premises. The paparazzi been swarming my crib ever since Vee and I broke up, so the fewer people I've got coming in and out, the easier my life becomes."

"Ah, yes, I understand," lied Miss Paletsky.

"So I was thinking," Seedy continued, contorting his face into an overwrought "thinking" expression, "that Melissa's piano teacher could live in our second guesthouse. That *you* could live in our second guesthouse. You know . . . if it wasn't too inconvenient."

"This is a very appealing proposition, Mr. Moon."

"Seedy," he corrected.

"Seedy"—she blushed—"and I would love to help nurture Melissa's newfound affection for classical music. However, I cannot. You see, in two months my work visa, she expires, and I return to Russia."

"Well, can't you teach Melissa until then?"

Miss Paletsky scratched her shellacked head in contemplation. *But, no!* What was she thinking? She could not move into the Moon home!

"I don't think Melissa should have a teacher who will abandon her so soon," explained Miss Paletsky.

"Well, then," Seedy shrugged, preparing to bluff, "looks like she won't have a teacher at all."

"Why is this? I can give you the name of so many teachers. I will find Melissa a——"

"It's no use, Lena!" Seedy bellowed suddenly, with a quick chop of his bejeweled left hand. (Miss Paletsky couldn't help but notice the appealing bareness of his ring finger.) "Melissa says she will only take lessons from you. It's really too bad. I always wanted to have another musician in the family." He shook his glossy bald head at the apparent injustice. "Guess some things just aren't meant to be. . . ."

Seedy Moon's sad face was unbearable. The way his perky posture dissolved into a tragic hunch, the way he cast his kind black eyes down toward the blue classroom carpet. And oh, my goodness! Was he actually pouting? Yes, Seedy Moon's bottom lip was pressed forward with the exaggerated appearance of a sulking child who has been denied a slice of chocolate babka. It was too much to bear.

"I will do it, Mr. Moon." Miss Paletsky nodded quietly. "Please do not be so sad anymore. I will do it."

Seedy's pronounced pout quickly snapped back into that

luminous grin. *Phew*, thought Miss Paletsky.

She met his shining eyes with her own, only briefly, and then glanced at her desk. Finally, Seedy broke the silence.

"Melissa is going to be so happy," he said.

The Guy: Evan Beverwil
The Getup: Brown and beige board shorts from ZJ
Boarding House, white Stüssy t-shirt, green Havaianas
flip-flops, white Turk's head bracelet

"I can't do Baja Fresh again, dude," Joaquin Whitman announced. "Like, can. Not. Do. Baja. Fresh."

It was lunchtime, and as always, Joaquin and his glassy-eyed comrades were taking longer than anybody else to leave the Showroom, having stopped for an impromptu game of hacky sack outside Joaquin's purple and yellow VW bus.

Theo launched the green and gold crocheted orb high into the air, and Brendan Hearne caught it on the back of his neck. With a fliplike motion of his tangled blond curls, he shot it back into the air, where it proceeded to hit Evan Beverwil square in the head and plop to the ground.

Evan jumped, surprised, causing Brendan, Joaquin, and Theo to dissolve into peals of laughter. Theo was famous for his deep intense laugh, which sounded like Old Man River guffawing into a megaphone. Joaquin giggled like a girl.

"Dude, you are the most out of it right now," Brendan told Evan, between cackles.

"Yeah, what'd you do, wake-and-bake before school or something?" Theo inquired.

"No," began Evan. "Or, uh, yeah."

cute little boot
Mohawk General
Store

That, of course, cracked them up even more.

"You know you're faded when you're so faded you don't remember getting faded," Brendan sagely announced.

"Speaking of getting faded," Theo began, pointing at the place on his wrist where someone who cared about time might wear a watch. "Ticktock."

"Okay, let's bounce," Joaquin declared. Theo popped the back door of the VW open and slid across the sky blue torn vinyl seat.

"Your turn to ride shotty," Brendan told Evan, climbing into the backseat beside Theo.

"Naw, it's all you," Evan mumbled. "I'm gonna chill on campus today."

"Dude, what?" Brendan wrinkled his brow. "You stayed on campus yesterday."

"Yeah, what, you don't smoke anymore?" Theo inquired.

"Or what, you don't eat anymore?" Joaquin pressed.

"Yeah, dude, are you, like, anorexic?" offered Theo.

"Yeah, he's, like, manorexic," Joaquin agreed.

Evan pushed some air between his lips, waving them off. "Whatever you say, dudes."

"Evan, calm down, man, it's okay," Theo assured him. "We still love you. Even though you're manorexic."

"See you in fifth period, dickheads," Evan laughed, shaking his head so his sandy golden locks swayed in the noonday sun. Then he made a break for it.

Evan still had five minutes till he was supposed to meet Janie in the projection room, so he dipped into the men's room to look in the mirror. He liked what he saw. His hair was doing that thing where it sort of crashed into a wave over his left eye and looked all shiny, too. He'd washed it with this stuff he stole out of Charlotte's bathroom. It came in tiny green bottles, and it smelled really good. Like, too good maybe. Damn, did he smell like a chick? It was the first time Evan had ever used conditioner and it made his mane all — well — glossy, which is what it had said on the bottle. "Glossing conditioner." Yeah, he'd read the bottle. Even the directions.

He wanted to do this right.

While he was sudsing the fragrant green goop into his ocean-stiff hair, Evan had thought about the thing he was thinking about right now. Which just so happened to be the thing he was thinking about while he attempted to do his Chem homework the night before. And while he skateboarded with Theo after dinner. And, well, every other minute of every day since the Pink Party, and a lot of minutes of a lot of days before the Pink Party too. Her, man. Janie Farrish. He hadn't liked a girl this much since, well . . . ever.

Evan smiled at his reflection in the mirror. Aside from the shiny hair part, he looked like he didn't give a shit, which was exactly how he wanted to look. Just some old green flip-flops, some brown and beige board shorts, and a threadbare white Stüssy shirt. The retro one, with the big sloppy logo. He was ready. Evan exited the bathroom and started for the projection room, unconsciously quickening his flip-flopped step.

"Hi, Evan!" chirped whatsherface and her one friend with the hair as he whizzed by.

"Sup," he replied, with a quick, upward jerk of his chin. He was on a mission. Nothing would derail him.

Evan got to the projection room before Janie, and saw the pile of *Godspell* programs they'd totally knocked over during their last brutally hot make-out session all splayed out on the floor. Clearly, nobody had been in there since they had. Which was awesome, like their private little sanctuary remained untainted, like a holy site. That was the bulletin board Evan had pressed her up against, the rickety table where she'd pressed up against him, and the light switch he was going to switch off after Janie Farrish came walking through that projection room door in all her smoking hot Janie Farrish splendor.

Any minute now . . .

Evan checked his cell. 12:27. He'd asked her to meet him at 12:20. Oh, well. Maybe she was, like, getting ready or something. Evan cupped his hand over his mouth and nose and checked his breath. *Sick.* He pulled a stick of Big

Red out of his backpack and started to chew.

12:28. Evan wasn't sure where to sit. Should he just be standing there when Janie walked in, or was that sort of weird? Should he sit on the stool? Yeah, he'd sit on the stool. Or did that look even weirder? Like the way they made you pose when you took those dreaded class pictures every year. Like, sort of perched. Yeah, the stool was weird. Evan stood up again. He could be reading when Janie came in. That would look casual. But he only had textbooks in his backpack, and if he was standing there perusing a textbook when Janie came in, that would probably be even weirder than if he was perched on the stool. This sucked. He could be texting when Janie came in. That would look cool. Not to mention normal. He whipped out his cell. Again.

12:29??

Evan quickly tired of fake texting and emerged from the dark room on the off chance Janie had thought she was supposed to meet him in the theater itself, and not the projection room. Negative. The theater was empty, save for some wiry dude with a fro, standing on stage performing a monologue to an audience of zero.

12:31.

Maybe their text messages got, like, crossed?

"What are we doing today?" asked Juliet, popping a ranch-flavored Soy Crisp into her Lipglass-slathered kisser. Crumbs of green-flecked seasoned salt stuck to the gloss while she chewed. Then a gentle wind wandered through the breeze-way, adding a strand of her hair to the mess.

"We're going shopping at the Grove," Carly announced, puncturing her Vita Coco box with a short pink straw, and regarding her friend's mouth with disgust.

"Oooh, yay!" trilled Juliet. "I heart the Grove! Where are we meeting?"

"Nikki's house," answered Carly, folding her black harem pants—clad legs Indian style.

"I can't today," replied Nikki, lifting her Red Bull suggestively. "I'm on the clock."

"What?" demanded Carly.

"Poseur stuff," clarified Nikki.

"But it's Fri-day!" whined Juliet. "And you've already worked, like, eleventybillion hours this week!"

"Fashion never sleeps, bitches," shrugged Nikki. "Emergency recon."

"*En ingles*?" Carly rejoined.

"Well, I really shouldn't be getting into this, but Melissa assigned me this top secret research project. I have to find out everything — like, *everything* — about the designers of this t-shirt brand called Schizo Montana. My job isn't done till I have their birth certificates. And Melissa does not accept photocopies."

"Wow, intense much?" marveled Juliet. "Why does she need all that?"

"I'd rather not say," Nikki answered.

"Translation: 'I have no clue why she needs all that,'" mocked Carly.

"Of course I know!" Nikki bristled. "Melissa shares everything with me. It's just not for y'all's ears."

"Nikki," Carly began, crinkling her concealer-caked forehead and staring straight into her traitorous bestie's cornflower blue eyes, "I know you're lying right now. You totally have a tell."

"I do?" squeaked Nikki, in awe of the casual way Carly tossed around poker lingo. "What is it?"

Carly waited patiently.

"Okay, fine," Nikki began. "I don't know why Melissa wants me to find out about Schizo Montana, but I *do* know that she would never put me on such a hard-core mish unless it were super important."

"Thank you. That wasn't so hard now, was it?" Carly inquired. "Oh, and b-t-dubbs, you don't have a tell."

Bitch!

"I'm just having a Scorpio moment," Carly shrugged. (Carly had recently discovered she was born on the Libra-Scorpio cusp, instead of squarely in Libra territory like she'd always thought, an astrological distinction she believed justified virtually any social injustice.)

"Nikki, darling," Carly continued, "Juliet and I are beginning to have some — well — *curiosities* about your internship. We have been listening to your accounts of the various duties you perform, and we have been paying particular attention to your alleged 'friendships' with your employers, and—"

"We don't believe you!" blurted Juliet.

Carly smiled a slow evil smile: "Precisely."

"You are always like, bla-di-bla, Melissa complimented my belly chain, and la-di-la, Petra smoked me out, but we've never even seen any of them talk to you!"

"That seems peculiar to me too, Juliet," agreed Carly. "Does it seem peculiar to you, Nikki?"

Nikki's eyes felt sore and a familiar lump was beginning to form in the back of her throat. She always felt exactly the same thing when she was about to burst out into tears. *No, dammit! Do not let evil Scorpio lady win this round! Do. Not. Cry.* But there was that same old gummy taste in her mouth, that telltale pressure behind the eyes . . .

And then something miraculous happened.

"Hey," interrupted a decidedly postpubescent male voice.

Nikki, Carly, and Juliet turned in tandem to see the surf god of Winston Prep leaning against the cracked theater door. He had on this white t-shirt that brought out the bronze color of his skin. Yeah, bronze. He looked like he was actually *carved* out of bronze. Or wait — did you carve bronze or, like, pour it into a mold? Whatever. This guy, this god among men, looked like he was *made* out of bronze, however you made it. And the sun was right behind him, framing his impossibly chiseled face like some kind of astral halo, and his hair . . . his hair was actually glistening!

Nikki dropped her California roll; Juliet wet herself, but just a little; Carly's nips were totally on fire. It was Evan Beverwil — *Evan Beverwil!* — and he was talking to *them.*

God, look at these fetuses, he thought, eyeing the blond one. She kinda stood out in those shiny pants and that jewel necklace thing around her stomach, and he was pretty sure she was the chick he'd seen floating around with the Poseur girls, bringing them coffee and shit.

"Was Janie, uhm, Farrish . . . was she here?" he asked. Carly and Juliet shook their heads, too stunned to speak.

"I'm pretty sure I saw Janie's car leave the lot," Nikki answered in her most enunciated voice. "Of course, she and Jake share the Volvo."

"Yeah!" chirped Juliet.

"Yeah, they do!" confirmed Carly.

"So, you're saying maybe you saw *Jake* leaving campus in the Volvo?" Evan confirmed.

"Maybe," Carly concurred.

"That's a totally good point," Juliet agreed.

"Except," Nikki recalled, "Jake was in Charlotte's car at lunch. They went to Kate Mantilini. So it must have been Janie that left campus in the Volvo."

Evan frowned. "Oh," he grunted, letting the theater door swing closed behind him. "Okay."

"Do you want me to tell Janie you're looking for her?"

Evan paused and then shook his head. "Nah. It's not, like, important." And with that, he loped off toward the Showroom.

The Nicarettes clutched each other, imperceptibly vibrating, and squealing at a frequency nobody — save bats and a few breeds of dogs — could hear.

The Girl: Janie Farrish
The Getup: About to get much better . . .

"I'd like to return this shirt, please?" Janie cleared her throat, holding the offending tank at arm's distance like a dirty Kleenex.

"Okay," the Ted Pelligan salesgirl mumbled, plucking the silky green garment from Janie's outstretched hand and shaking it out. She was the same salesgirl as before, but her star-lashed amber eyes betrayed no sign of recognition, and so — instead of complimenting her Afro, which twinkled today with glitter — Janie kept quiet, examining her nails.

She felt a little better already, just having that cursed green top out of her possession. 'Cause it was the exact same chlorine green color as Evan's eyes. Those eyes that had seemed so adoring that night by Melissa's pool, that day in the projection room; those eyes that had so *enraptured* her as they locked with hers.

God, how blind could one girl be!

Janie had actually thought Evan might like her, when all along, he was really just thinking about how *repulsive* it was to kiss her. Or maybe what Janie did with her mouth couldn't even be *called* kissing. Maybe it was so gross that it didn't even *classify* as kissing. But if Evan was so disgusted, why had he gazed at her like she was some kind of goddess? Oh God . . .

maybe that was just the way his face looked all the time! All milky and lovesick. Maybe that was the face he made no matter what was happening, even when he was thoroughly repulsed. Like when he tasted spoiled milk. Or stepped in dog doo. Or kissed somebody seriously repugnant.

Janie's scuffed navy Samsung vibrated in the pocket of her Cheap Monday skinny jeans. It was Amelia. Pretty much the only call she would answer right now.

"What a *jerk!*" Amelia erupted in greeting.

"Whatever," mumbled Janie, picking at a frayed cuticle. "I mean . . . it's not his fault I kiss like a, like a . . ."

"Stop!" ordered Amelia. "You do not kiss like that. And by the way, what straight dude talks to his sister about how some chick kisses anyway? Seriously, Janie, that seems kind of gay to me. It sounds like he's not attracted to girls, but since he's this manly surfer dude, he has to pretend he is, so to get out of having to be intimate, he makes up some weird lie about the girl he's dating and spreads it around to—"

"Spreads it around!" gasped Janie.

"Okay, scratch that part," amended Amelia. "But seriously, Janie, he sounds gay to me. Didn't you say his room was covered in shells or something?"

"He's not gay."

"Then why does he spend all his free time paddling around on an eight-foot phallus?"

"*Melia*," Janie pleaded, her lips forming something

vaguely resembling a smile for the first time all day.

"Seriously, Janie, screw Evan Beverwil. There are gonna be so many hot guys at the Troubadour on Friday, it's gonna be obscene. Like, it's actually gonna be *disgusting* how many sexy, brooding, tattooed guys come out to this show. Older guys. Older *musician* guys. All you have to do is show up looking crazy-hot — which you always do anyway — and we will douche this douche nozzle out of your system for good, alright? I will not permit you to get all sniffly over some dude who listens to *Bob Seger!*"

By now, Janie was full-on grinning. When it came to her particular brand of misery, Amelia was better than Prozac. "Can you please consider a career as an inspirational speaker?" Janie begged. "Because you just made me feel approximately five hundred percent better."

Janie looked up from her ravaged cuticle to find that as her mood had skyrocketed, the salesgirl's had nose-dived in equal measure; she looked seriously miffed.

"Lemme call you back," Janie said, and clicked the end button. "Sorry about that."

"Yeah," replied the salesgirl. "So, this tank you bought? It just went on sale, so you can't return it. I can either give you store credit or you can exchange it now."

"I," Janie announced, puffing up with a peculiar feeling of invincibility, "will exchange it now!"

The salesgirl looked at her like she was deranged, but

Janie didn't care. She was royally hopped up from Amelia's speech, and she was gonna find some ferocious new threads to wear when she showed up to the Troubadour on Friday night and flirted with one of those brooding-tatted-musician guys Amelia was talking about . . . or at least some ferocious new threads to wear while she gawked at them.

Janie spotted an amazing gold sequined minidress on the mannequin. It had a dainty layer of white chiffon at the hem and neckline, and a racerback, Janie's favorite cut. She located the dress on a nearby rack and eyed the relevant tags: designer (Gryphon), size (S), price ($570). She put it back on the rack. With tax, a $570 dress would bring Janie perilously close to her $1,000 spending limit. Plus, she still needed shoes, not to mention accessories. Janie's vision of her first, super-cool entrance at the Troubadour did not include her usual Converse and gummy bracelets.

Janie's cell vibrated in her purse. She figured it was Amelia again and fished it out. She figured wrong. It was a text message from Evan.

@ BAJA FRESH

At Baja Fresh? *At Baja Fresh?* Great! Here, Janie had thought she would be able to reclaim some shred of her dignity by "forgetting" to meet Evan in the projection room, and the guy hadn't even shown! He probably assumed Janie was in that dank little windowless prison right this instant, just twiddling her thumbs like some simpering loser. She pictured Evan sitting at Baja Fresh eating a stupid quesadilla with his stupid mold green eyes and his stupid frog-shaped toes, making stupid jokes to his stupid friends and imagining that she was actually stupid enough to be waiting for his stupid ass in the projection room.

Ooh! A slinky sleeveless silver dress with an awesome tiered skirt and zip-up back caught Janie's eye. Relevant tags: "Doo.Ri"; "Size 4." Irrelevant tag: "$995.00." In her first act of reckless abandon since conception, Janie pulled the grotesquely overpriced garment off the rack and tossed it over her arm. And once she'd broken that seal, there was no going back. Janie raced through the store, as ravenous and giddy as a binge eater in an overstocked pantry. She grabbed a caramel-colored leather jacket by Mike & Chris, a slouchy lace blouse by Stella McCartney, a leopard-print skinny belt by YSL, an asymmetrical bandage dress by Rodarte, a velvet bustier by Marc Jacobs . . . it was shopping porn, and Janie was seriously turned on. Every time she filled her hungry hands with another helping of couture candy, the salesgirl whipped over and transferred her booty to a nearby fitting room, leaving Janie to stock up anew. She was on fire. There were so many options!

Finally, Janie headed for the changing room, snatching up a pair of knee-high, black Christian Louboutin spiked-heel boots on her way. They were so beautiful Janie wanted to cry. But she didn't. Instead, she tore off her pill-ridden vintage V-neck sweater, kicked off her Steve Madden gladiator sandals, wiggled out of her Cheap Monday skinny jeans, and started trying on the most luxuriant garments that had ever touched her pale white skin.

Twenty minutes later, Janie marched out of the dressing room cradling a pile of leather and zippers and studs. The telltale red soles of the Louboutins dangled beneath the mound of fabric.

"I'll take these," Janie announced, heaping her dream wardrobe onto the pristine white counter. Then she motioned to the ocean blue velvet bustier she was wearing. "This top, I'd like to wear out." Janie had left her nubby old V-neck sweater — along with her nubby old self — back in the changing room, suffocating under a faux fur vest by Rebecca Taylor.

The salesgirl snipped the tag off Janie's new favorite shirt and scanned the remaining items, folding each with origami-like precision and wrapping them in tissue paper before dropping them into a Ted Pelligan bag; the large one this time, with the stiff cardboard bottom and the braided rope handle.

"This skirt is bananas," gushed the salesgirl, folding a tiny square of black cotton into an even tinier pellet. "We just got it in." Janie was silent.

"That will be $3,480," beamed the salesgirl.

Whatevs.

Dogfish handed over the card.

The Guy: Ted Pelligan
The Getup: Gray twill vest and trousers by Penguin,
lavender-and-white-striped button-down by Paul Smith,
navy boat shoes by Sperry, pink paisley ascot with
matching pocket square, colorless mani/pedi

Wendy Farrish was . . . bemused. Sitting beside her, in one
of the lushly upholstered green velvet chairs in Ted Pelligan's
Melrose office, was Bud Beverwil, the ultimate multi-
hyphenate. Not only was Bud an Academy Award–winning
actor, but he also wrote, directed, and produced. Plus, he
just so happened to be an avid art collector, a triathlete, and
the impossibly glamorous husband of the impossibly glamorous, chlorine-eyed ex-model Georgina Malta-Beverwil.

Georgina Malta-Beverwil sat in a cushioned wicker
chair at her husband's side, fishing for something she never
seemed to find in her quilted Chanel tote. *What movie had
Wendy seen her in back in the eighties . . . ?* She couldn't quite
remember. And neither could anybody else. But that didn't
really matter, because for the last decade and a half, Georgina had been playing her most famous role to date: Bud
Beverwil's wife.

Today, however, Georgina had come to Ted Pelligan not
as Bud Beverwil's wife, but as Charlotte Beverwil's mother.
She was here, with Charlotte's classmates' parents, to talk

to Ted Pelligan about the launch of her daughter's latest little hobby. *So what was her plastic surgeon doing here?* Yes, Georgina was positive that was Dr. Greene hunched behind the antique maple highboy, tapping away on his BlackBerry Storm. Dr. Greene's wife, Heather, appeared to be as far from her husband as space permitted, leaning against the wall near the polished wood door.

Heather had panic attacks sometimes, and standing near exits calmed her down; she liked knowing she could escape quickly, should the need arise. But Heather didn't think she'd have to make a break for it today. She'd popped half a Xanax on the car ride over, and plus, Ted Pelligan: Melrose was her sanctuary. She spent at least two days a week shopping here. She actually bought the lavender Juicy Couture sweatsuit she was wearing today at Teddy P's. After the meeting, Heather planned to reward herself with some lite shopping downstairs, followed by a Bloody Mary in Ted Pelligan's shady outdoor café. There was no place she felt more at home, including, tragically, her actual home. Heather pulled a turquoise elastic off her bony wrist, swept her ash-blond hair into a high ponytail, and gazed amorously at Seedy Moon. *Now, that's a man. . . .*

Seedy Moon was looking as dashing as ever, dark smooth skin contrasting handsomely with his white-on-white Adidas tracksuit. The amber ceiling light glistened softly against his just-shaved head, and Seedy smiled a small peaceful smile, like he had found some secret to joy that nobody else knew.

Dr. Robert Greene was not feeling quite so serene. "Hey, folks, how 'bout we get this show on the road, huh?"

That's when a dreidel-shaped man with a pink paisley ascot popped out from behind the tall velvet curtain.

Wendy Farrish, who was sitting closest to the curtain, gasped in surprise. Georgina Beverwil clapped her manicured hands, amused.

"Hullo!" exclaimed the jowly newcomer. "I am Ted Pelligan." And with that, he wobbled over to the massive mahogany desk. With his unplaceable British-ish accent, immaculate silver eyebrows, and vintage pocket watch, Mr. Pelligan seemed transported from another time. But he looked perfectly at home in the aggressively antique office. In stark contrast to the spare modernity of the store downstairs, Ted's office — from the finely bound, never cracked first edition books that lined the ceiling-high bookcases to the antique maps mounted on the eighteenth-century fleur-de-lis wallpaper-lined walls — was an absolute time warp.

"You must be Petra's parents," Ted intoned, eyeing the man with the Blackberry and the woman in purple terry pants. "Your daughter is a rare and beautiful bird. You," he told Bud and Georgina Beverwil, "must be Charlotte's parents. Your daughter reminds me of Audrey Hepburn, before I made her who she is today. And you!" he told Seedy Moon. "You must be Melissa's father. That girl has more fire than a dragon with a vendetta." Then Ted noticed the lady in the turquoise cat's-eye glasses. "And you . . ." he began, crinkling his freckled forehead so his long gray eyebrows met in the middle.

"Janie — Janie Farrish's mother," Wendy said.

"Yes, of course!" Ted replied, with a dramatic "silly-me" slap to his blotchy forehead. "Jamie's a lovely swan. A lovely, lovely swan, I tell you."

"Janie," Wendy corrected.

"So," Ted continued, sinking into the brass-studded burgundy wing chair behind his humongous desk. Ted's chair was so low and his desk so high that once he sat down, the parents could see only his thick white hair, floating over the slab of mahogany like a dollop of cream. "Your daughters have created a beautiful product," he began, cranking his chair to a higher level. "As I'm sure you all know by now, I came across the Trick-or-Treater bag through a fortuitous accident, and became enamored on sight. We at Ted Pelligan have since begun production on one thousand copies of the enchanting parcel, with many more in the pipeline after that. Once the Trick-or-Treater lands in stores, I have no doubt it will replace everything from the Kelly bag to the Hefty bag."

"That's great, Ted — can I call you Ted?" bellowed Robert Greene from his spot by the antique maple highboy. "But I just want to know how you plan to keep these kids from squandering all that loot."

"Could you repeat the question, my dear sir?" Teddy rejoined, fluttering his short silver lashes perplexedly.

"Well, take our daughter Petra for example," Robert explained. "She says you are giving her — what is it? — fifteen grand to produce this purse? And that concerns me, concerned parent that I am, because I know my daughter is not responsible enough to cart around that kind of dough."

"You don't trust your own daughter?" Wendy inquired.

"Not particularly, no. And even if I did, I still think that us parents deserve a slice of the pie here, right? No, I'm kidding. But seriously, between the private school and the ballet lessons, that kid *has* practically sucked us dry."

"Robert," Heather whispered, "Petra has not taken ballet since—"

"I just think," Robert interrupted, "that it makes a hell of a lot more sense for us responsible adults to handle the money stuff ourselves. Let the kids focus on the sewing." (The self-proclaimed "responsible adult" did not go on to mention that he had invested — and lost — half his family's assets in a Ponzi scheme earlier that year.)

"No disrespect, Mr. Greene," Seedy began, "but nobody in this room is touching a dime of my girl's share. Melissa may be a teenager, but she is also a savvy businesswoman, and I intend to treat her like one."

"I think I agree with Mr. Moon," nodded Wendy. "The

girls were responsible enough to create a product that is actually being produced and sold in stores. Surely they are responsible enough to handle the profits that product brings in."

"I think there's been a misunderstanding here," offered Heather. "Sometimes it's hard to tell when Robert is kidding. The man has quite the poker face. I assure you he's just teasing when he talks about controlling Petra's share."

"The hell I am," mumbled Robert.

Bud Beverwil's iPhone belted out an emotive Puccini aria and he leaped up from his velvet chair. "Tell me something good, Marty," he barked, walking into the hallway and leaving the heavy polished door wide open.

"Listen," Robert began, trying in some small way to repair his rapidly dwindling image in the eyes of the other parents. "I'm sure your kids are different. Especially you," he assured Seedy. (Hello, Robert was a jerk, but he wasn't stupid. He'd heard Seedy's new song about throwing that lady in the L.A. River.) "But Petra just isn't responsible enough to handle that kind of cash flow. She'd just roll it up and smoke it."

"Is that a metaphor?" Wendy pursed her lips.

"Well, no. I mean, yes, I guess technically it's a metaphor because she won't roll the money itself up and smoke it, right? But no, 'cause it's not a metaphor for something other than smoking—" Robert was confusing himself now.

"She'll spend it on drugs," he clarified. Then he shrugged. "Look, we've got a bad seed on our hands."

"Bad seed. Sad seed. Glad seed. Fab seed," Ted Pelligan mused, making a tiny tower with his chubby pink fingers and affecting an air of pensiveness. He did this often during meetings when he wanted to change the subject, repeated somebody else's statement over and over until it lost all meaning and then went on to talk about whatever he wanted to talk about. Which, in this case, was the girls' image.

"These little lovelies are each so different. Each so original. Each so unique," Ted began. "This is becoming an issue. I invited you all here today so that you could sign off on the project, of course, but also because I wanted to get a look at the people who spawned these delicious creatures, so I might better assess the best direction to take their collective image in the months to come. And I am learning a lot." Ted inspected the lady in the horrific Juicy suit, as glassy-eyed and sylphlike as her daughter; Seedy Moon's commanding presence was perfectly replicated in Melissa; and the chlorine-eyed model was as fabulously unimpressible as her pocket-size daughter, Charlotte. As for that lady with the glasses, she exuded a wry, perceptive quality that was the essence of her daughter.

"Jesus, not again!" bellowed Bud Beverwil from the hall. "What the hell do you mean, she's been hospitalized for dehydration? You're busting my balls, Jerry! You're busting my . . . Yeah? Well, you tell Gabrielle if she's not on set in the next *hour* I am replacing her today. (Pause.) Nobody is irreplaceable! (Pause.) I don't care if we're over budget on reshoots. This is art! This is not business, you pea brain, this is art!"

After one of Bud Beverwil's infamous on-set tirades was caught on tape and released to TMZ a few weeks earlier, his publicist had insisted he stay away from the set of reshoots for his new film *Dead on the Vine* until he completed anger management. But Bud had been away from the set for two days and he was already eating himself alive. A guy drops the f-bomb once or twice, and now he's sentenced to spending the remainder of his days in some creepy library talking about his daughter's sewing class? No thank you. Bud loved Charlotte and all, but this meeting was taking the whole "father" thing a bit too far.

"I'm on my way," barked Bud, "and you tell Gabrielle Good that if she is not on set by the time I get there, not to bother coming back. (Pause.) Then get her some water! I'll see you in ten."

Teddy's office had gone quiet. It was difficult to talk over all that yelling. After a few beats it was clear that Bud was not coming back.

"Well, then, let's continue?" Georgina Malta Beverwil offered finally, affecting breezy unawareness of her husband's outburst.

"Certainly," Ted agreed. "Giddy!"

Ted Pelligan's deliriously somber right-hand man, Gideon Peck, appeared soundlessly in the doorway. "The contract, sir," Gideon announced, head bowed, his tone as weighty and apologetic as a doctor telling a patient he has two weeks left to live.

"Splendid, bring it here," Ted intoned.

Gideon crossed the room in long slow strides, keeping his eyes trained on the Persian rug all the while. He presented a document to his gourd-shaped superior and then produced a gold Montblanc from the pocket of his Dolce & Gabbana tuxedo jacket. Then, with an even deeper bow of his already bowed head, Gideon made his exit.

"So," Ted began, "the last step in our little powwow today is for you all to put your John Hancocks on this here slip of tree, so we can get those Trick-or-Treaters into select stores as soon as possible. It's a rare thing indeed for this sort of contract to be signed by the *parents*, and not the designers themselves, but *quel* can I *do*? Your precious saplings are ahead of the curve. Just think," he sighed, clasping his small hands. "To have all your dreams fulfilled at such a young age! To be famous!"

The lady in the peculiar glasses met his exclamation with a strange and fretful expression. Mr. Pelligan laughed, extending his Montblanc.

"Madam?"

The Girl: Melissa Moon
The Getup: Current/Elliot Love Destroyed boyfriend jeans, white Splendid V-neck t-shirt, black lace La Perla push-up bra, white gold Rolex, pink Uggs, Glow by JLO perfume

"What are you doing over there, baby?" Marco Duvall called from across Melissa Moon's high-ceilinged birdcage-shaped bedroom. It was halftime, and Marco had finally turned away from the Lakers versus Celtics game to find his girlfriend still hunched over her gold-trimmed princess desk, poring over a stack of documents.

"Lissa!" Marco repeated, chucking a frilly, corn dog–shaped pillow at his annoyingly studious girlfriend.

It hit her square in the ponytailed head — he had great aim — and landed at her pink Ugg-clad feet, causing Emilio Poochie, the toy Pomeranian who'd been slumbering there, to leap up, clearly annoyed. And E-Poo wasn't the only one.

"Marco! Can you not see that I am *working*?"

"Okay, okay, chill," mumbled Marco, from his nest on the overstuffed bed. "I just thought we were gonna watch the game together."

"Well, the game is on, and we're together."

"Yeah, baby, whatever you say," answered Marco, stretching so his Winston Falcons jersey lifted to reveal his flawless, b-ball-toned abs. Melissa didn't even look his way. Damn. He couldn't stretch forever. He tried a different tack.

"I'm starving. You want to take a break and make me some of Melissa's famous mac 'n' cheese?"

"No, Marco, I do not," Melissa snipped. "I have a lot of homework and I really don't have time to take a break."

"A'ight," shrugged Marco. "It's cool. I'll just starve." He eyed Melissa for a response — anything — but her espresso brown eyes remained trained to the pages in front of her and showed no signs of budging.

"You can't take one day off?" Marco whined.

"Nope," Melissa snapped back. "Not unless it's Christmas, New Year's, or Usher's birthday."

Marco gave up and headed downstairs to fashion some sort of crude snack himself. He was perpetually starving; Marco ate every hour, and he could kill a quart of milk in a single sitting, but he never gained a pound.

Melissa pushed her pound cake–colored Chanel reading glasses up the bridge of her smooth straight nose and reread the page in front of her for the gazillionth time. Nikki Pellegrini had done her research. She had found out every possible detail about the founder of Schizo Montana. From his name (Ariel Berkowitz), to his shoe size (7), to his Bar

Mitzvah venue (the FOX lot), Nikki had left nothing out.

So why wasn't she satisfied?

She opened her MacAir and clicked on SchizoMontana .com, which she'd added to her favorites yesterday for easy viewing. More like *least favorites*. There he was on the home page, that Ariel Berkowitz punk, grinning this dopey smug smile from beneath his lame ironic mullet. His multicolored fluorescent clothing was garish against his pale, scrawny body, and black-rimmed geek glasses framed his eyes.

Melissa clicked on the "About Schizo Montana" link, even though she'd read it so many times she could recite it by heart:

Schizo Montana is a clothing line that celebrates a true Santa Monica original. If you've spent any time on Montana Avenue, you have experienced the unique charms of Ms. Schizo Montana, a homeless woman who traverses the Avenue, alternately cawing like a bird and cursing George Bush. (Yeah, we tried to tell her there's a whole new White House regime, but yo: she won't listen.) Our line is a celebration of this L.A. mainstay, with each limited edition tee featuring one of Schizo Montana's many personalities. And no, this isn't exploitation, so don't bother asking! We are totally tight with Ms. Montana. We love her and she loves us too.

Melissa clicked on the "Shop Now" tab and zoomed in on a wife beater silk-screened with a photo of a homeless woman wearing a petticoat over her pants. She was seated alone at a table outside the Coffee Bean & Tea Leaf, talking to herself. The words "The more, the merrier!" were printed across the bottom. Melissa felt physically ill. Poseur had not just lost the *Nylon* cover to a t-shirt brand. Poseur had lost the *Nylon* cover to the single stupidest t-shirt brand in the history of fashion.

Melissa couldn't contain her hatred any longer. She clicked on the "Contact Info" tab, cut and pasted Ariel's e-mail handle, and then clicked over to her own e-mail account — Divalish16@gmail.com — and immediately started typing.

Dear Mr. Berkowitz,
Congratulations! You have created the single most offensive clothing line in the history of clothing lines. And no, I don't mean offensive in some cool, Eminem/Howard Stern kind of way. I mean offensive as in offensive to my eyes because it is so empirically ugly. So, good job! Thanks for making L.A. an uglier place to live in with your lame-ass merchandise.
Toods,
Divalish16

Melissa hit send. She was pulsing with anger; high on

it almost. She clicked back to the home page and stared at Ariel's smug smile again. Puke. She couldn't see his eyes well enough though, so she dragged the photo to her desktop and blew it up using Photoshop. Magnified a hundred times, Ariel's eyes were warm and alluring. *Just like Satan's*, Melissa thought.

She clicked over to her Gmail account to reread her clever e-mail, and found, to her surprise, a response from the fluorescent Satan himself.

Divalish, Wow:
You really are pathetic. Seriously, do you have a life at all? Or do you just troll around the Internet looking for things to comment on all day? I bet you're a forty-year-old woman with nineteen cats and no boyfriend, and you just finished your box of Franzia wine and John Mayer is playing in the background at your tiny apartment right now and you're desperately lonely and sad because John isn't singing about you so you go online and send hate letters to people like me. People who have real lives and do cool stuff and actually leave their houses and go out into the world once in a while. Okay, go make out with your John-Mayer-shaped pillow!
Peace out, biatch,

Ariel

Oh. No. He. Did. Not.

In a single pulse, Melissa read the entire e-mail again, managing to get even more pissed off the second time. She sat up stick-straight in her champagne velvet upholstered office chair, cracked her knuckles, and furiously started typing.

Oh hey, Ariel,
That is such a cool-ass name, yo. Are you, like, the Little Mermaid, or something? Are you totally in a bad mood 'cause your stinky-ass va-jay-jay's stuck inside a flipper? Well, you can chillax, baby girl! Prince Eric saves you in the end and then you get to go on land and trade in your seashell bra (which I'm sure you fill in nicely by the way) for one of your hideously moronic t-shirts.
Say hi to your crab(s) for me!!
Love,
Miss Divalish to You

Melissa hit send. Then she read her e-mail over, cackling aloud at every jab. Well, that was that. She closed her Mac and took her biology book out of her pink Juicy tote to do some real work. But when she tried to read a page of bio, she failed miserably. She stared at a diagram of the stages of mitosis, but fluorescent Satan's crooked smile was all she could see. Melissa couldn't handle it. She had to know if he'd responded. Melissa popped open the computer once again, and sure enough, he had already replied.

Dear John Mayer lover,
Uh, yeah. You need therapy.
Ariel

Melissa clicked the reply button.

I need therapy? This from a dude who considers making fun of mentally ill homeless ladies the epitome of a good time?

Send. Melissa drummed her tan hands on the gold-trimmed princess desk, jaw clenched. Then she hit refresh. Nothing. Then she hit refresh again. Nothing. Then the response came:

You're right. You're obviously too cracked-out crazy for therapy. Maybe you'd like to be featured on our next t-shirt?

"Eew, sick!" called a voice from the doorway. "I think

this milk has gone bad." Melissa turned to see Marco holding a quart of buttermilk in one massive mitt and a bag of Pirate's Booty in the other.

"Marco, that's buttermilk!" Melissa scolded, slamming her computer shut again. "You are not supposed to drink that. It's for Emilio Poochie! I give it to him as a treat when he's good."

Marco ambled toward the princess desk, slow and sultry, trying his best to smolder, and knelt down in front of Melissa so they were face-to-face. "And what treat do I get when I'm good?"

"Marco Duvall," Melissa chided, "I do not walk onto the basketball court while you are in the middle of a game and try to get sexy with you, do I?"

"No," Marco replied with a sly smile, "but I wish you would."

"This!" Melissa continued, motioning to the space around her executive desk with her tan, smooth hands, "is *my* basketball court. I'll let you know when it's halftime." As Melissa huffed and puffed, her perky double D's jiggled and bounced inches from Marco's still-smiling face. Well, that was something at least. . . .

She had told him long ago that she was "waiting for marriage," and Marco respected her for that. He could wait. But weren't there, ya know, other things they could do to pass the time till then? They'd been dating for four months, after all. Marco was one of the best athletes at Winston Prep, but when it came to Melissa, he had yet to round second base.

Marco sighed. "Kiss?"

Melissa leaned forward so he could see straight down her V-neck to her black lace La Perla push-up bra and planted a quick peck on his lips. Marco rose, placated for the moment, and headed back to his nest on the overstuffed bed with his Pirate's Booty and buttermilk. He unpaused the Tivo.

"Li-ssa!" sang an approaching voice from the white marble staircase. "I got good ne-ews!" Seedy Moon appeared in the doorway beaming.

"Yo, Mr. Moon, how goes it?" asked Marco.

Seedy's smile dissolved at the sight of Marco and his buttermilk mustache reclining against his daughter's ornate cream and gold Louis XVI headboard. "Whattup, Cafeteria," he muttered, before turning back to Melissa. "I said I have good news, baby."

"What is it, Dad?" sighed Melissa. "I am really busy right now."

"Well, you're gonna want to hear this, trust me. I paid a little visit to Lena today, and with some excellent acting if I do say so myself, I managed to convince her to become your piano teacher. She's agreed to move in!" Seedy chuckled proudly. "So you better start appreciating classical music, girl!"

"That's good, Dad. That's really great!" Melissa chirped, happy but preoccupied.

"'That's *good,* Dad. That's really *great?*'" Seedy laughed. "I thought you'd be losin' it you'd be so excited."

"No, I am, Daddy," Melissa nodded, spastically tapping her pink-Uggs-clad foot.

"At first," Seedy recounted with theatrical flair, "she was all, 'No! I cannot! My visa's up soon and I must return to Russia!' So I said — right on the spot! I thought of this right there! — I said, 'But Melissa said she will only take piano lessons if they are with *you!*'" Somehow, Seedy managed to pull off both a very bad impression of Miss Paletsky's Russian accent and a bad impression of his *own* accent. His Seedy Moon voice was actually worse than his Miss Paletsky voice.

"So then, she said, 'I will do it, Mr. Moon,' and I said, 'Melissa is going to be so happy.'"

"And I *am,*" grinned Melissa. "Don't you believe me, yet?"

"Okay, I believe you," nodded Seedy. "Catch you later." He saluted and left.

"Catch you later, Mr. Moon!" Marco bellowed after him. Silence. *Damn. The Moon family sure did love to shoot him down.*

Melissa popped her abused laptop open again and started brainstorming a response to Ariel's last jab. But it didn't take long for guilt to set in. Melissa never acted bratty with her dad like that. And normally, she would have been so pumped about Miss P agreeing to move in. What was her deal? All Melissa could think about was that damn mermaid and his stupid mullet. Seriously, it was like an addiction.

Maybe she really did need therapy. . . .

The Girl: Charlotte Beverwil
The Getup: Porcelain ruffled Kate Spade blouse, black pencil skirt and maroon velvet blazer by Theory, grandmother's cameo brooch, Christian Louboutin lace and button booties

At that same moment, in a therapist's waiting room across town, Charlotte was eagerly awaiting her first couple's counseling session with Jake. Dr. Hortense Bonnaire's office was right behind Le Pain Quotidien on Melrose, which, though not the most authentic French restaurant in the city, still appeased Charlotte.

Jake bought a chocolate croissant there to eat in the waiting room.

"This was a good idea," Charlotte trilled, laying her tiny smooth hand on Jake's corduroy-clad knee. Charlotte looked like a true miniature lady for the occasion, with her glossy black curls gathered into a low chignon, a frilly off-white blouse, and a maroon velvet blazer with the cameo brooch affixed to the lapel. As she perched on the delightfully beautiful and remarkably uncomfortable couch, tearing little shreds off of Jake's croissant (and kind of wishing she'd gotten her own), Charlotte was as happy as she could be. Because for once, she was as French as she could be without actually leaving the boring old U.S. of A.

Jake smiled. "If we don't like it, we don't have to come back," he said, more to himself than to Charlotte. The whole French existential therapy thing had seemed so suave at first, but now he was having second thoughts. What if the doctor didn't *get* the whole Nikki Pellegrini thing? What if she turned Charlotte completely against him?

What if this was the stupidest idea he'd ever had?

The blond wood and stainless steel door opened, and standing there in a black turtleneck and gray pleated slacks was Dr. Bonnaire. She was six feet tall at least, her black hair sliced into an angular bob streaked with gray.

"Come in," she announced.

Charlotte and Jake followed Dr. Bonnaire into her stark, charcoal-colored office and sat down on a couch as stiff and beautiful as the one in the hall. Their brand-new therapist lit a cigarette and settled into a chair that looked like a wooden crate. Charlotte instantly recognized the piece from French minimalist darling Philippe Starck's infamous Crisis collection.

"So?" asked Dr. Bonnaire, her accent so thick that even the word *so* dripped in French-ish-ness; Charlotte was ecstatic.

"So, hi," Charlotte began, "I'm Charlotte Beverwil and this is my ex-boyfriend, Jake Farrish."

"Why do you come to tara-pee with an ex-boyfriend?" asked Dr. Bonnaire, eyeing the couple unsmilingly while her cigarette smoke slowly filled the sealed room.

"Well, we are hoping to become less 'ex' and more 'boy-friend,'" Jake explained, before adding, "also girlfriend."

"And so you think zis *sing* — zis *romance* — will fill zee hole you feel inside?" Dr. Bonnaire inquired to nobody in particular.

"Yup, that's what I'm hoping," Jake replied.

Charlotte shot him a glare, and he mouthed *what*, sitting up straighter.

"Do you love zis person?" Dr. Bonnaire asked Jake.

"What?" he sputtered. Right after he went blind and deaf.

"Do. You. Love. Zis. Person?"

"Well, um, we haven't, like, said 'I luh, I luh . . .' But, you know. It certainly isn't out of the question. I think."

"Zen zis is good," replied the doctor, gracefully exhaling another lungful of smoke. "You will make Uncle Zam very 'appy."

"Uncle Zam?" Jake bristled. "Excuse me?"

Dr. Bonnaire yawned aloud, as though Jake's very existence bored her to the point of exhaustion. "I will tell you two zomething that will sound very harsh to your ears, but that you must know. If you want to know zee truth, that is. Do you want to know the truth? Or do you prefer to be like zee —what is it" — she searched for the word — "or do you prefer to be like zee lemmings?"

"No, we want to know the truth," Charlotte assured her, fiddling with her brooch and feeling unsure.

"Okay, then," Dr. Bonnaire began, crushing the first of many Gauloises into a matte ivory white box and leaning back in her wooden crate. "Romantic love does not exist. *Comme le pipe, n'est pas?* Romantic love eez your Zanta Claus. It eez your fairy for zee teeth. It eez zee capitalist construction used to keep zee American lemmings busy while zare president takes zee country to war. *Zare eez no romantic love.* Zare is only sex. And war. And finally, mercifully, death."

Charlotte tipped her china cup chin perplexedly.

"Um, Dr. Boner, I'm sorry but I'm going to have to disagree with you on that one," Jake began. "Unless . . . is this, like, some sort of hazing process you do before you actually help us, or something?"

"What is zis?" Bonnaire frowned. " 'Ow you zay, 'ayzeeng?"

"What Jake means," clarified Charlotte, "is it's difficult to believe all the stuff you just said . . . about how love is the tooth fairy and all — you know?"

"Oh, 'av I upset you?" She laughed, croaking like a toad in a bog. " 'Av I caused you *distress*? As difficult as it eez to 'ear zeze sings, once you 'ave come to terms with the nothingness of life, of your zo-called love, of your very existence, uh? Only zen will you finally live zuh *truth*. But . . . ," she sang. "Maybe you are not ready for truth?"

"No, we're ready for truth!" Charlotte insisted. "Jake," she nudged him. "Tell her how we're ready for truth."

Wow. Kissing Nikki Pellegrini had now officially been bumped down to the *second* worst idea Jake had ever had; because coming here today was definitely, unequivocally, the worst.

"People cannot cope with their irrelevance, their littleness," mused Dr. Bonnaire, "and so they try to find meaning where none exists, by manufacturing myths like religion. And the only myth more pathetic than religion is love. But you are not here to learn these things, are you? That is not why you have come today. So let us talk about your relationship. About your 'love.' What went wrong?"

"Well, Jake cheated on me with this eighth-grade whore, Nikki Pellegrini," Charlotte explained, "and now I can't decide whether or not to get back together with him because maybe he will just do it again and also because it was so humiliating."

For the first time, the deep vertical lines above Dr. Bonnaire's mouth stretched taut and her teeth showed between her painted lips. She was smiling. The expression looked garish and strange on her usually somber face, like a crazy clown.

"Jake broke zee rules!" Dr. Bonnaire exclaimed.

"Yeah, exactly!" agreed Charlotte. "Jake broke the rules."

"And whose rules are zoze?" pressed Dr. Bonnaire.

"Well, the boyfriend-girlfriend rules," Charlotte replied, confused. "*Everybody's* rules, I guess."

"Zay are not my rules," said Dr. Bonnaire. "Zay are not Nietzsche's rules. Zay are not Camus's rules. Zay are *your* rules."

"I don't follow," admitted Charlotte.

"Your sense of right and wrong is your own creation. Morality is merely a fool's attempt to ascribe meaning to the choices we all make each day. But how can a choice have any meaning when all of existence is meaningless?"

"So, Charlotte should just get over the whole Nikki Pellegrini thing," Jake summed up.

"Yes," agreed Dr. Bonnaire. "Charlotte should 'get over' it. And you should 'get over' Charlotte. And you should also 'get over' using 'love' to escape the truth, which is—"

"Lemme guess," Jake interrupted, "that nothing means anything anyway."

Dr. Bonnaire shrugged assent.

"So, riddle me this, Boner," Jake began, perking up in his seat. "Why do penguins mate for life? Are they just trying to find meaning where there really is none? 'Cause I don't think penguins are complex enough to do all that. How do you explain their instinct toward what can only be described as love?"

"Zee penguins," chuckled Doctor Bonnaire. "People

always bring up zee penguins. Two penguins can make the heart shape together with their beaks, and so *quoi*? People sink zey are in *love*."

"No," Jake rejoined, beginning a long and futile attempt to illuminate Dr. Bonnaire on the intricacies of penguin mating rituals that proceeded to eat up the remainder of the session. Finally, thankfully, the good doctor cut him off.

"*Ah non!* It is time," Dr. Bonnaire announced. She stubbed out a final Gauloise in the matte white box and rose to escort the couple out.

"Can I just ask you one last question," Jake began when they reached the blond wood door. "Why do you even bother working as a therapist if everything is meaningless anyway? Or for that matter, why do you even get out of bed in the morning?"

Dr. Bonnaire nodded. "The truth eez everyone is bored, and devote d'emself to cultivating 'abits." Then she smiled that freaky clown smile. "Camus," she confessed.

"Yeah, well maybe you should give up the therapy thing and find a different 'abit,'" Jake rejoined. "Like making lanyards or something."

"Good-bye," said Dr. Bonnaire. "Call me to schedule another session. Or don't." Then she closed the door.

Back at the Volvo, Jake discovered he had gotten a parking ticket. Forty-five dollars. Lovely. He started the car, but then turned it off and looked at Charlotte, who was curled up in the passenger seat as far away from Jake as physically possible, staring out the grimy closed window. The words WASH ME were printed across it backward in a childish scrawl.

"Before we go, I just want to say—"

"Jake," Charlotte interrupted, without even turning her head. "Just drive, okay?"

Wow. So this was really it. He had really lost her. Jake turned to face forward and cranked the key in the ignition.

They were off.

The Girl (sort of): Don John
The Getup: Plaid Burberry shorts, nude Hide & Sleek Spanx cami (shhh . . .), red Modern Amusement tee, clear Baby-G watch, gladiator mandals

When Charlotte strolled into her backyard at 7 p.m. that Friday for some "twi-bathing," her brother Evan was already on his fifty-fourth lap, and counting. Evan was one of the lucky few that dealt with depression not by shopping, binge drinking, or shoveling entire jars of peanut butter down his gullet, but by exercising. And exercising. And exercising. Since Janie flaked on their projection room date one day earlier, Evan had already run seven miles, surfed for four hours, and swum fifty-four laps — wait . . . fifty-five! — in the Beverwils' Olympic-size pool. So why didn't he feel any better?

An equally lovelorn Charlotte laid her Gucci beach towel on a lawn chair and sprawled out, for once, sans reading material. Twi-bathing sans *Vogue* was usually as unthinkable to Charlotte as steak au poivre sans pommes frites, but she just couldn't focus today. And so the gorgeous Beverwil siblings cradled their respective agonies in shared solitude, while melancholy Erik Satie music poured out of the rock-shaped speakers. That is, until . . .

"Poo-kie!" wailed a painfully peppy voice from behind the ivy-covered fence. "Where be-ist thou?"

Charlotte goes twi-bathing

aviators protect from the harsh moon rays

Vintage Kimono wrap

ERES (rhymes with heiress) bikini

Lanvin Rose blossom sandals require chlorine water daily, and plenty of moonlight

Janie Farnish

There were sixteen beeps, followed by a loud buzz and the steady purr of an electric gate opening. Ugh, why had Charlotte given Don John the key code? She really could not handle him right now. Or anybody else for that matter.

Don John skipped like a doe across the fresh-cut grass to the foot of Charlotte's lawn chair and gasped.

"Eres!?" he intoned. "I die!" Don John was referring, of course, to Charlotte's dazzling midnight-blue Eres bikini.

"Eres indeed," Charlotte confirmed, slipping her massive Oliver Peoples Ballerina shades down over her eyes, despite the fact that it was dark out.

"So, you'd better get changed," Don John began, "unless you're wearing that to *la cinema*, which, b-t-dubbs, you totally should. But in the event that you do not want to see *Pierrot le fou* in a bathing suit, chop-chop!"

"*Pierrot le fou*," Charlotte repeated. *Merde.* They'd had plans to see the film for weeks because a) Charlotte adored French New Wave cinema, and b) Jamie, Don John's gorgeous copper-headed acting-for-television teacher, also adored French New Wave cinema, which *had nothing whatsoever to do with the purely coincidental fact that* c) Don John suddenly adored French New Wave cinema.

But there was no way Charlotte could sit through a movie right now. She was far too enchanted by her own misery for distractions. "I'm really not in the mood right now," she said. "Rain check?"

"*Quelle tragédie*," Don John exclaimed, barely conceal-ing his mirth. He kicked off his gladiator mandals, slipped his newly pedied feet into Charlotte's gold Dior thongs, and asked, "so where should we go instead? It's Friday, so Social Hollywood will be off the hook, but Mike and Mike promote Tropicana Bar at the Roosevelt Hotel on Thursdays, which means we could totally get in, and then we could sneak into Teddy's through the back entrance! Or we could do Hyde? But I really think Hyde is going downhill. Last time I went, Jeremy Piven was the only celeb there, and every girl in the bar was stuck macking on him. It was really depressing. Actually, that guy from Sum 41 was there too, and he's actu-ally much cuter in person, P.S., but he was there with Avril, so obviously he was off-limits. Did I ever tell you about how Avril stood up on her chair and started dancing?"

"Yes."

"Oh. Okay, so anyway, I'll give you my top three and then you give me yours. Mine are Social, Teddy's, and Bar Marmont. Oh, wait, and Winston's! Can I have four?"

"You can have as many as you want, DoJo, I'm not going out." Charlotte flipped onto her stomach to sun her back in the dark.

"Eew, why?"

"Because I have a big decision to make and I need to think," Charlotte replied.

Don John kicked off Charlotte's thongs and pouted.

What was it with people always thinking *alone*? Couldn't they think *and* party?

"A bunch of people are going to the Creatures of Habit show at the Troubadour later if you want to do that," she offered. *Also,* she thought, *he can report to me on Jake, who will totally be there.*

"Creatures of Habit?" Don John inquired.

"It's a band," Charlotte explained. "Kind of punk rock."

Don John actually shuddered. *No, thank you.* He'd rather dance in an empty 7-Eleven parking lot to the sound of a distant car alarm. He was fully prepared to tell Charlotte precisely that, too, *except*, he realized in awe, *Evan was emerging from the pool.* Was it just Don John or did that boy actually walk around in *slow motion*? The twilight shone against Evan's impossibly chiseled abdomen, illuminating the water droplets that clung there like morning dew. He looked like Ryan Gosling without the totally distracting and therefore entirely unnecessary DARFUR t-shirt. Evan looked even tanner than he had earlier that day. How was that possible? Had he *not* just been swimming in the dark? But Evan had that gift, he guessed. Just when he got as tan and blond and generally godlike as a guy could get, he got a tad tanner, a bit blonder, and just a touch more generally godlike.

Instead of reaching for one of the fluffed and folded towels in the bamboo hutch behind Charlotte's chair, Evan shook off like a frisky golden retriever, soaking his sister and her gawking sidekick in the process.

"E-van!" whined Charlotte, scrambling up to sitting.

"*E-van!*" he mocked. "You know you're outside, right? By a pool? You're supposed to get wet."

"There's this great new invention called a towel," Charlotte rejoined, plucking a chartreuse Ralph Lauren beach towel from the always stocked hutch and chucking it at her dripping brother. "Learn it, live it, love it."

Evan roughed his sandy locks with the towel, then tipped his head to the side and smacked it to knock the water out. "Hey," he inquired, balling the towel in his fist. "Were you guys just talking about Creatures of Habit?"

"Yeah," Charlotte replied.

"Janie's friend is in that band."

"So?"

"So, I don't know." He frowned. "I've actually been meaning to check them out."

Charlotte narrowed her eyes in suspicion behind her oversize shades. "You know they sound nothing like Bob Beaver or whatever, right?"

"*Seger*," Evan corrected, rolling his chlorine green eyes. "So when are they playing?"

"Ten," Don John informed him.

Evan nodded, chucked his wet towel at his prissy sister, and headed for the French double doors.

"I'll come with you," Don John volunteered. "You

shouldn't be left alone with those troub-boobs."

Charlotte shot him an accusatory glare.

"What?" he defended himself, bugging out his Bette Davis eyes. "You *said* you needed to think. And besides," Don John sniffed. "Evan'll need a wingman."

The Girl: Miss Paletsky
The Getup: Knee-length stonewashed denim skirt, purple Merona turtleneck sweater, "suntan" L'eggs pantyhose, black suede Capezio pumps, sterling silver dangling sun and moon earrings

It was too much. This couldn't really be the *guesthouse,* could it? Miss Paletsky looked down at the key in her small, pale paw; the key that dangled from a silver heart-shaped Tiffany key chain; the key that had been waiting in an envelope marked "Lena" underneath the doormat of Moon Manor; the key to her new life.

The Moon guesthouse was so luxurious that Miss Paletsky feared she was dreaming, only she knew she could not be; for she did not possess the imaginative capacity to conceive of such gorgeous design, such plush fabrics, such glistening surfaces, such magnificent artwork, such complete and utter unfettered luxury. . . . So this really was the *guesthouse*?

Miss Paletsky's new home was a microcosm of the main house where she had once played piano for Seedy Moon. It boasted the same slate-tiled floors, imported from Africa, the same original Warhols, and the same impossibly spare modern glamour that characterized Moon Manor.

She headed for the bedroom to put away her floral-print

rolling suitcase, and there she espied the most lush, regal bed she had ever laid eyes on. The all-gold bed was so high that one had to mount a custom-carved wooden ladder to reach it. It was a bed for a king! And yet it was a bed for Miss Paletsky. She ran her delicate, pale hand over the Frette duvet cover, and pressed gently. Her hand sank into the most decadent feather bed money could buy. Miss Paletsky felt like Dorothy when she wandered into the field of poppies, eyelids heavy. If she climbed that hand-carved ladder, if she peeled back those 400-thread-count sheets, if she sank into that foot-deep feather bed, Miss Paletsky feared she might never get up again.

Before she could even entertain the idea of entering that pristine bed, she needed to take a shower. Miss Paletsky located the bathroom, which wasn't hard, since the bathroom in its entirety was visible from the bedroom through a wall of barely frosted glass. Even the toilet! Miss Paletsky couldn't help but blush.

She bid the king-size bed adieu — but only for now! — and headed for the shower. As she crossed the threshold into the bathroom, the temperature changed rapidly from the perfect 68 degrees of the bedroom to a carefully calibrated 75. More comfortable for undressing, which Miss Paletsky promptly did. She stripped off her casual-Friday ensemble — a stonewashed denim skirt, a purple turtleneck sweater, and "suntan" L'eggs — and dropped it into a deep bamboo hamper. She stepped into the doorless, curtainless shower and turned the lever, releasing a torrential downpour from two bowl-shaped showerheads.

Using a watermelon-size sea sponge, Miss Paletsky lathered her body with one luxuriant product after another. The shampoos and conditioners and salt scrubs and soaps, all aptly named "Bliss," scented the room with sour lemon, cleansing sage, warm vanilla, tangy blood orange, and spicy pepper. As Miss Paletsky scrubbed and scrubbed, it was as though all of her sad memories and toxic stresses were disappearing into the invisible drain beneath the cedar planks. Gone was her past with Yuri, her pending return to Russia, her unrequited love of Seedy. For the first time she could remember, as the warm clear water stroked her tired body like a baptism, Miss Paletsky wept from happiness.

She turned off the shower, stepped through the cloud of fragrant steam, and reached for the cleanest, whitest, plushest Egyptian cotton towel she had ever seen. Wrapping herself in the giant bath sheet was like the hug Miss Paletsky had needed so badly since her tumultuous arrival in America. And then she saw, hanging on a pink silk hanger, an impossibly beautiful white cashmere bathrobe. Miss Paletsky touched the sleeve of the garment and recalled with astonishing clarity the only other time in her life she had felt such softness. As a young girl, her mother had once taken her to a pet store, and she had held a bunny rabbit so soft and white that she refused to put it down until her mother forced her to, making her cry as they left the store.

Could she put this bunny rabbit robe on her body? Miss Paletsky was ecstatic at the thought. *But no!* She quickly realized it didn't belong to her. Miss Paletsky turned to leave the room, but the mere thought of leaving the robe behind almost brought her to tears. She had no choice. She slipped the lush fabric off of the silky hanger and wrapped her orchard-scented skin in the luxurious garment, cinching the belt around her slender waist.

Clean, revived, refreshed, and giddy, Miss Paletsky wandered through the guesthouse. Beneath a several-paneled painting of Marilyn Monroe, Miss Paletsky found a remote control the size of a paperback, with a series of buttons, switches, and lights as varied and complex as the controls on an airplane. She flipped one switch, and heard a humming sound above. A panel of the ceiling rolled away to reveal the ink-black, star-splattered sky. A gust of crisp night air rushed in, chilling her warm skin so the dainty hairs on her arms stood up. Miss Paletsky found the brightest star she could and closed her eyes, like she had so many nights before. But for once, she could think of nothing to wish for. And so she only whispered, "*Spasiba.*" Thank you.

Miss Paletsky pressed another button, and a glass orb in the middle of the room filled with lush orange flames. Then she flipped a switch and heard the sound of a babbling brook. Was this sound coming from hidden speakers, or had Miss Paletsky just turned on an actual river? It was all so impossible that anything was possible! Another button caused a sixty-four-inch plasma screen to levitate out of the floor. But what use was there for television when life itself was such a fantasy?

When Miss Paletsky wandered into the kitchen, the slate tiles felt warm against her clean bare feet. Was it possible that the *floor* was even heated? Miss Paletsky knelt and pressed her hands to the deep gray tiles. Her heart rose into her tiny palms. They were actually warm! Miss Paletsky felt so strange and silly and elated that she closed her eyes, laid her tiny chipmunk cheek against the heated floor, and laughed aloud. When she opened her eyes, she spied the edge of something shiny and black through the door, not unlike the water-slick river stones that bordered the shower. Curious, Miss Paletsky rose to inspect the next surprise. A shiny black sports car converted into furniture, maybe? A human-size bust of Seedy Moon, carved out of onyx perhaps?

But once Miss Paletsky entered the room in question, she found something far more magnificent than a Lamborghini-turned-coffee table. She found a piano, and not just any piano: a Steinway grand. Whose was it? And would they mind if Miss Paletsky sat down on the glossy, smooth seat, just for a second? She didn't even have to play it. She just wanted to *sit* on that seat. And what harm could that do?

But once Miss Paletsky slid down the smooth, glistening

bench, her hands seemed to lift the piano lid of their own volition, and soon enough, she was running her fingers over the gleaming white keys. And then, it was only a moment until . . .

Ping!

She pressed a single key. The note was perfectly pitched, beautifully clear; like an ivory elevator door in heaven sliding open. She couldn't contain herself. As though possessed, Miss Paletsky pressed another key. Flawless. And another. Gorgeous! And before she knew what had hit her, Miss Paletsky was swaying amorously from side to side, her tiny hands dancing over the smooth white keys. She could have played forever. Miss Paletsky lost herself in the music and became so transported, in fact, that she did not even notice the gentle rap on the open front door. Or the way Seedy Moon crept inside and stood behind her while she stroked the keys. She did not notice, that is, until she did.

"Oh!" Miss Paletsky called in fright.

Seedy chuckled a low, steady laugh. "I'm sorry, Lena," he said in that silky voice that was even smoother than the notes on the Steinway. (*Seriously!*) "I didn't mean to disturb you."

Miss Paletsky counted the humiliations:

1. Seedy had caught her playing the piano without asking.
2. Seedy had caught her wearing the bunny rabbit robe without asking.

3. *She was wearing a robe!*

"I just wanted to check up on you. Make sure you were settling into your new digs okay. How's everything looking so far?"

Miss Paletsky gazed into her stocky savior's smiling eyes and forgot all about her gaping robe. "Everything is perfect," she sighed. Then she remembered — and clutched it closed.

"So, what were you playing?" Seedy asked.

"Prokofiev."

"Huh. I've been struggling with the bridge for this new song I'm working on, and that tune you were playing kind of gave me an idea." Seedy motioned toward the empty space on the bench beside Miss Paletsky and inquired, always the gentleman, "Do you mind?"

Do I mind? thought Miss Paletsky. *Do I mind if traveled from class to class on a cloud of vodka vapors?* But Miss Paletsky didn't say that. Instead, she only shook her head no.

Seedy smiled and slid onto the bench beside her. Miss Paletsky scooted over to give him space, but they were still close enough that they were almost touching. Then he reached his strong hands over the keys and began to play the opening bars of his latest tune. Miss Paletsky tried to focus on the music and not on the intoxicating closeness of this man, this tightly bound package of muscle wrapped in smooth dark skin whose mere proximity woke her up like a jolt of electricity. Breathe in, she reminded herself. And out. In . . . Out . . .

"So, right here," Seedy said, interrupting Miss Paletsky's emotional combustions, "something like that Prokofiev thing. Not the first part, but the, ya know . . ." Seedy began to hum, and Miss Paletsky instantly recognized the melody he wanted. She nodded comprehension and played the bridge with her right hand.

"That's it!" he exclaimed. Miss Paletsky blushed, giddy like she'd won a prize. "Play it again," he instructed, and Miss Paletsky's fingers flew across the keys. While she played her part, Seedy closed his eyes and nodded, absorbing the tune. "Again," he whispered when she reached the end, and Miss Paletsky played the bar again. Seedy, still nodding, reached for the keys and began to riff off of her, his low notes diving into her high ones and bringing them down to earth. When they reached the end of the tune, Seedy kept playing, improvising in low, sultry notes. Feeling brazen, Miss Paletsky chimed in with some high notes, and a slow steady smile crept across Seedy's face while he continued to play. He led. She followed. He hung back. She took the reins. He followed her lead. Then, drunk on the moment, Miss Paletsky lurched into the low register just as Seedy reached for a high note. Their arms touched, the keys mashed — *ching-ka-plunk!* — and Miss Paletsky jumped back, embarrassed.

But Seedy didn't look embarrassed.

"That was cool," he nodded.

"Yes," agreed Miss Paletsky. "And the song you wrote is very beautiful. What is it called?"

The song was called "What You Done." It was the last installment in Seedy's latest trilogy about Vivian's betrayal: "What You Do," "What You Did", and "What You Done." When he turned to answer her question, Lena was so close he could almost smell her. Like orange tree leaves and cinnamon. Wow. Like morning.

"It's called 'What You . . .' " He trailed off. Miss Paletsky gazed into his eyes.

"Yes?" she prompted. He inhaled. Cupcakes. Exhaled.

"Uh . . . 'What You . . .' doin' for dinner?"

The Girl: Vivien Ho
The Getup: Mourning garb: black Diane von Furstenberg feather-embellished Thane dress, black Wolford tights, Yves Saint Laurent Tribute platform sandals, oversize black-on-black Fendi shades, and the omnipresent Ho Bag

The sushi platter was positively prismatic. A thick slab of ruby red tuna drooped over a warmish cube of sticky white rice, three hunks of yellowtail sashimi glistened like rose quartz, and a dainty ribbon of seaweed surrounded a pile of translucent yellow fish eggs, which glistened like just-cut amber. The thick blob of wasabi, of course, was the color of money.

A wooden chopstick plunged toward the decadent spread and impaled a quivering baby octopus. It then lifted the briny morsel to a collagen-injected kisser, slathered needlessly with BlingFusion After Hours lip plumper. The grease-slick lips belonged to none other than Vivien Ho. Contrary to popular belief, Seedy Moon's infamous ex was alive and well. Or she was *alive* at least; the jury was still out on the *well* part.

Ever since the six-foot Korean stunner with the violet eyes (which she *swore* were not color contacts) and the yard-long stick-straight shiny black hair met rapper-cum-producer Seedy Moon on the set of his "Lord of the Blings" music video, the pair had been inseparable. Vivien was a backup dancer, but she managed to strategically place herself to catch Seedy's eye, and soon enough, she was engaged to the hip-hop heavy and living in his Bel Air palace, with everything she'd every wanted within snatching distance. She started her own handbag line — Ho Bag — which had already branched out into apparel, and her memoir, *The Audacity of Ho*, had just been released in paperback. A perfume — working name Just Ho — was in the sniffing stages, and her manager was shopping around a reality show about Vivien's newlywed years with Seedy (although he didn't know that yet). She'd had it all.

And now it was all gone.

Vivien masticated the baby octopus slowly, her violet eyes far away. Her shopping bags, however, remained close by. She had popped into Neiman Marcus on her way to Urasawa that evening for yet another dose of Rodeo Drive retail therapy, but no matter how many chinchilla shrugs she charged to her Visa black card, no matter how many jewel-encrusted Manolo Blahniks she acquired and then promptly forgot about, no matter how many size 8 Dior cocktail dresses she bought and then had her assistant sew in a size 4 tag, nothing could console her.

Vivien missed Seedy Moon so bad it hurt.

And now, just because she'd played an innocent little

trick on his daughter, Melissa, Vivien was stuck alone at Urasawa, with nothing but a $250 platter of sushi to catch her tears. If she ever happened to shed any.

But even though Vee lacked the ability to cry or otherwise express human emotion, she was still all torn up inside. Here's how it all went down, as anybody who had visited a single gossip blog in the last week already knew: Vivien's soon-to-be-stepdaughter Melissa couldn't come up with a name for her fashion line (*and how hard was that, really? Vivien Ho had thought up the ingenious name Ho Bag without outside assistance*), and so Melissa and her little "colleagues" included a Name Our Label contest as part of their launch party. For reasons that continued to evade Vivien, over one hundred people showed for the bash. Each and every attendee scrawled a potential name on a clothing tag and dropped it into the huge clear globe that served as the centerpiece for the soiree. Later on, when nobody was around, Vivian snuck in and changed every last submission to the word "Poseur."

Melissa threw a fit when she cracked open the globe and discovered the stunt, and so Seedy set out to apprehend the saboteur. He hated to see his little girl upset. Vivien wasn't worried though. She'd covered her tracks perfectly; or so she thought. Eventually, and against all odds, Seedy had managed to crack the code. His Koreatown private eye took on the case and found traces of sea kelp on every last tag reading Poseur. *Sea kelp?* Seedy thought his K-town wizard was losing his magic at first. Until he caught a glimpse of the ingredients in Vee's lotion one day, that is. Numero uno: *Seaweed*. Seedy didn't want to believe it, but in the end he had no choice; at the famed Pink Party, in front of everybody they knew and plenty of people they didn't, he called off the engagement.

First, Vivien attempted denial. But when that failed, she caved, confessed, and begged Seedy to see her side of the story. She explained that it had all been a misunderstanding, easily attributable to temporary insanity, brought on by an excess of acid in the system. You see, Vivien had been on the Master Cleanse Diet for two weeks when she sabotaged Little Miss Princess's little contest, meaning she had subsisted for fourteen days on nothing more than lemon juice, cayenne pepper, and maple syrup. Sure, one could drop twenty pounds in two weeks from the acidic bevy, but one could also go mildly insane. It was a seriously serious diet with totally legit health risks, both physical *and* mental. So you see, Vivien had not been herself at all when she pulled that little prank on Lissa. She'd been a woman under the influence.

As somebody who had never done the Master Cleanse, however, Seedy was tragically unsympathetic. He kept insisting that even if Vivien *was* temporarily insane from her diet, she still should have confessed to the sabotage after the fact.

But how could Vivien confess after the incident when she had *no recollection* of the incident! Because along with temporary insanity, yet another (undocumented) side effect of the Master Cleanse was *amnesia*!

Vivien felt so sorry for herself she could cry. That is, if she could cry. Seedy would not listen to reason, and had insisted that Vivien had pulled the prank because she hated his daughter. His little princess. His Melissa. Which, of course, was ridiculous.

Vivien stared unblinking at another baby octopus, trying to will herself to cry. She affixed her gaze to the small, spiny tentacles and her vision blurred into a kaleidoscope of burnt orange and cinnamon brown. When her sight refocused, however, eyes still dry, Vivien was horrified. The octopus had Melissa Moon's face on its teeny-weeny brain head! And all eight tentacles were waving into the air, like "Talk to the hand, talk to the hand, aha-ha-ha-ha!"

Vivien speared the tiny bulb like a medieval warrior.

"Excuse me," called a nasal voice. Vivien snapped her violet eyes to the left to find a thirty-something blonde with rock-hard double-D's leaning toward her from a neighboring table. "You're Vivien Ho, right?"

It was Jocelyn Pill Brickman, studio mogul Bert Brickman's ex-wife. Today, like so many days, the former Miss December and Playmate of the Year had spent the afternoon trolling the shops of Beverly Hills with her two besties-sinceforevies: Pepper and Trish. The threesome was celebrating Jocelyn's fabulous appearance on *The View* that morning to promote her new book, *The Afterwife: You're Divorced (Not Dead!)*, and so they'd eschewed their usual single glasses of cabernet and gone for the bottle. Thus, Jocelyn was pretty far gone by the time she leaned over to the six-foot-tall black-clad stunner.

"Yeah, *so?*" Vivien replied. For once, she just wanted to blend in. In the days since the Pink Party, Vivien had been skewered by the media, and cast as some sort of evil nemesis to Seedy and his "poor unsuspecting daughter." (Access Hollywood's words, not hers.) In an attempt to repair her tarnished image, Vivien had even hired Lil' Kim's courtroom stylist, hence the seriously somber duds she was wearing today. Black, black, and more black. And not an inch of visible skin. To Vivien, any top did not allow her breasts to "breathe" was comparable to wearing a burka, but she had obeyed the stylist's advice. There was nothing Vivien wouldn't try right now.

Jocelyn smiled a cabernet-stained grin. "Don't worry," she whispered. "We hate that little high school skank, too!"

"*Hate!*" echoed Pepper, the unlucky one who got stuck having brown hair because Jocelyn had "called" blond back in high school, and Trish had quickly snatched up red. Pepper was convinced that her brown hair was the only thing preventing her from fully realizing her potential as a

Christian pop singer, but Jocelyn insisted there could only be one blonde in the group. *And you do want to be in the group, don't you?*

"Me-lis-sa," Trish winced, screwing up her face like she'd just tasted Lysol. "She had the gall to sit at our table at Mariposa one day. Seriously, *someone* needed to give that girl a reality check."

"A *fat* reality check," smiled Pepper, looking to Jocelyn for props.

"What Pepper and Trish and myself are getting at here, Miss Ho, is that you are our *idol*. You are, like, the Mother Teresa of Rodeo Drive, representing all the women who have been irritated by that little gnat."

"Wow," Vivien replied, cause hey, flattery would get you everywhere with her, "thank you. I really did take one for the team, didn't I?"

"Absolutely!" confirmed Pepper.

"You must come join us for a drink," Jocelyn exclaimed.

"We insist!" Trish chimed in.

"This cab isn't going to drink itself," Pepper agreed.

They didn't have to ask her twice. Vivien rose and joined their tiny table, and Pepper poured her a heaping glassful of wine. They watched, expectant, while Vivien enjoyed a long, slow swallow of the rich red medicine.

"Now," Jocelyn began, leaning forward so her man-made

mammaries were on full display. "Start at the beginning. And don't leave anything out."

"Okay," Vivien began. "It all started on day three of my Master Cleanse, which, as I'm sure you ladies know, is the toughest day of all." They nodded sympathetically. "So here I am, literally starving myself to fit into my eighteen-tier Vera, and Seedy starts talking about his daughter's little sewing class, and how she is going to throw a big party to name her lame little company. He would not stop talking about it! Ba-ba-ba, Melissa and her friends, and ba-ba-ba, fashion label, and then I find out the girls are having the party at the *Prada store*! Well, since the tension between Prada and my own couture label, Ho Bag, is well documented, it's obvious to me — and anybody with half a brain in their head — that Melissa chose the Prada store just to get my goat. And so I decide, *in my highly unstable Master Cleanse–induced state,* to teach Melissa a lesson. And so, when all those little twerps submit their proposed names for her 'fashion label,' I break in and swap out every last entry with the word 'Poseur.' 'Cause that's what she is. Just a little girl playing dress up." Vivien recoiled, surprised by her own venom (though not that surprised). "Anyway," she continued, "I tried to explain my side of the story to Seedy, but he just wouldn't listen."

"That is *so mean!*" Pepper whined.

"I know!" Vivien agreed. "He says he will never trust me again."

"Well, if there is one thing I know," smiled Joss, "it's divorce, and this guy owes you big-time if he calls off an engagement last minute like that. I know a lawyer who can get you a settlement you won't believe——"

"Oh, Seedy already gave me a settlement," Vivien interrupted. She gazed into her rapidly dwindling glass of cabernet and sighed. "He has been incredibly generous."

Pepper and Trish exchanged a look, perplexed. "Then what's the problem?" Trish intoned.

"The problem is," Vivien began, really wishing she could sob while she delivered her sob story, "the problem is that my reputation is ruined! You know that website GuessWhoDied.com? Well, after Seedy released that murder ballad, "Vivien," they pronounced me dead, and being dead has completely ruined my Ho Bag sales numbers. If things don't pick up soon, I will have to live like some kind of pauper! Eating at California Pizza Kitchen and shopping in malls!"

"Pull yourself together, Vivien!" Jocelyn demanded.

"I can't. Half of America thinks I'm dead and the other half hates me! I know the only way the public will love me again is if Seedy loves me first. I have to get him back! And plus" — she squinted her eyes hard and thought of her dead cat Noodles. Nothing —"I love him."

"Vivien Ho, we will not rest until you are Vivien Ho-Moon!" Pepper assured her.

"Yeah," Trish agreed. "We need a new philanthropic project anyway, 'cause the cleft palate kids are really played out."

"You are in good hands," Joss said. "Yossi and I have been married three times."

"Really?" Vivien inquired.

"Really," Joss replied. "Hey, what are you doing tonight, sweetie? The three of us are headed to the Transcendent Cream show, and there's one spot left in Trish's Range—"

"Transcendent Cream is this totally transcendent Cream Tribute band," clarified Pepper. "The best I've heard by a landslide."

"Especially when you want to feel, like, *mmm*! You know?" Trish added suggestively. Vivien managed to stifle her gag reflex.

"So, are you in or are you in?" asked Joss.

Not again, Vivien thought, eyeing the three remarkably taut, expectant faces before her. How was she always getting stuck in positions where she had to pretend to like music she hated? First, it was Seedy's jams (which all sounded exactly the same to Vivien: wack), then it was classical music (because isn't everybody cultured supposed to have classical music at their engagement party?), and now it was this . . . what? *Music to Perform Vaginal Reconstructive Surgery To?* Vivien shuddered. Why couldn't these women just listen to Fergie like normal people? But while "My Humps" played softly in the back of Vivien's head (*my lovely lady lumps . . .*) she eyed Joss, Pepper, and Trish and knew she had no choice. From the mountain of Neiman Marcus bags at their Jimmy Choo—clad feet to the suitcase-size Balenciaga bags that dangled from their chairs, one thing was clear as the flawless twenty-six-carat diamond she refused to remove from her ring finger: *bitches knew what they were doing.*

"I'm so in," she announced.

The ladies squealed, simultaneously raising their hands in the air. Having never had a friend before, Vivien was confused. But soon realized what she was supposed to do.

So she high-fived them each in succession and let out the best white-woman-dying-seal squeal she could muster.

The Girl: Janie Farrish? Or her smokin' hot older sister?
The Getup: Ocean blue velvet bustier by Marc Jacobs, black miniskirt with funky gold zippers by Preen Line, handcuff necklace by Juliana Eshaya, giant studded cuff by CC Skye, black knee-high Christian Louboutin boots

The band wouldn't be coming on for another ten, but the club was so packed you had to, like, *really* need to pee to justify the bathroom trek. All the chicks were dressed in a style best described as toddler chic: lacy baby-doll dresses, slouchy ankle boots, blunt bangs, and either torn tights or stripy thigh-highs. Eyeliner, smudged beyond recognition, completed the look.

Hours of preparation went into looking that messy.

But it was worth it because, he-llo? *This was the Troubadour.* You couldn't just show up like some geek off the streets.

Only one Creatures of Habit fan's I-don't-give-a-damnness came from the heart, and — *quel surprise* — she also happened to be the girl everyone looked at. Damn you, Petra Greene. With her cutoff jean shorts, braided hemp belt, and vintage silk scarf, ingeniously tied into a makeshift (and precarious) halter top, she was a study in effortlessness and cool. If she was an iHuman, she'd play something like Jeff Buckley's "Everybody Here Wants You," while everybody else played,"Beautiful" by Christina Aguilera, trying (and failing) to make themselves feel better.

Of course, what Petra lacked in effort, her date for the evening, Janie Farrish, more than made up for. The willowy girl with shy gray eyes had spent half the day absorbed in virgin sacrifice—worthy preparation, starting at the top and working her way down. She shampooed, blow-dried, and straight-ironed her hair into the sleekest bob imaginable, plucked her brows into perfect arches, painted her fingernails pitch-black, and outlined her eyes in so much kohl eyeliner she outsmoldered Bollywood, not to mention outaccessorized. Janie's swanlike neck and pale décolletage boasted the feminine-yet-completely-badass handcuff necklace she'd coveted all season, which (in case her wrist got jealous) she paired with the *Vogue*-featured gold stud CC Skye cuff, you know, *as seen on Eva Mendes*? Or AnnaLynne McCord?

Or Janie Farrish.

Of course, the accessories kind of paled in comparison to the main event: the clothes. Her narrow torso spilled into an asymmetrical chartreuse velvet Marc Jacobs bustier, and a black Preen Line miniskirt, replete with edgy gold zippers, hugged her slender hips, putting her long, toned legs on full display, aside, of course, from the portion covered by her polished black leather knee-high boots (Christian Louboutin, thank you very much). In her daring new Ted Pelligan threads, Janie looked like the girl she'd always envied and secretly wanted to be: cool, rebellious, and just a little dangerous. And isn't *looking* like the person you always wanted to be a tiny-yet-significant step closer to *being* the person you'd always wanted to be?

Janie was about to find out. And Jake could sling all the insults he wanted: nothing would steer her off course. She climbed into the passenger seat of the Volvo that night, ready for the sharpest of jabs. So when Jake announced, at the sight of her, "Nobody told me this was a Halloween party," Janie was ecstatic. "That's honestly the best you can come up with?!" she exclaimed. *Wow, turning into a badass was going to be way easier than she'd thought.*

They picked up Petra on the way and headed to the Troubadour. Then, as Jake pulled the car into an awesome street parking spot across from the venue, Petra informed him that she needed to talk to Janie. Alone. About her *period.* She didn't have to ask Jake twice. He turned off the Volvo and leaped from it as though ejected, reminding his skanky-looking sister to *lock up ol' Bess* when they were done.

But when Jake closed the door and disappeared from

sight, Petra didn't get into the age-old question of Tampax vs. DivaCups. Instead, she fished an Altoids box out of her hemp hobo and popped it open, revealing a lighter and a joint, rolled special for the occasion.

This was Petra's favorite part of the day. There was nothing like that first hit of weed, the way it entered your system daintily at first, and your brain stopped yapping, and there was only that sweet, soft high. As she exhaled that first toke, it was like somebody had taken the remote control of Petra's life and turned the volume down on all of her anxieties and stresses. And then, when she had taken enough hits, it was like they'd pressed the mute button. She enjoyed that part too; that utterly stoned, anything-is-funny-even–*Dude Where's My Car*, out of your mind high. When cereal tastes like Christmas morning and a Ben Harper song can change your life. Yeah, getting crazy high was cool. But for Petra, nothing beat that first drag. When reality just, like, receded . . .

"Don't babysit it."

Petra turned to find Janie staring back at her from the front passenger seat, cocking one impatient eyebrow. Petra burst out laughing. What movie was that from? Whatever it was, it was hilarious. But as she giggled and ran her fingers through her gloriously tangled honey blond hair, Petra soon realized that she was the only one laughing. And that Janie looked pissed.

"Sorry, I thought you were kidding," Petra explained, holding out the joint. "I didn't realize you blazed."

"Why?" asked Janie, pinching the spliff between her black-manicured fingers. " 'Cause I don't play hacky sack at lunch and think flax seeds are a food group?"

Janie placed the joint between her well-glossed lips and sucked hungrily, burning through a good half-inch of paper. It was quite the toke. Then she proceeded to die. Janie coughed harder than she had ever coughed in her life and her eyes filled with water. She coughed and coughed and coughed, and for a moment, she thought, *Okay, I will never stop coughing. This is just what I do for a living now. I cough. It is my occupation.*

"Are you okay?" Petra asked, gently patting Janie's back but knowing no amount of patting could remedy the hacking fit that was bound to follow an obviously amateur rip like that. Petra reached for the spliff and took a drag while Janie's coughs finally, mercifully subsided. Then, she cracked a window to let some smoke out; Janie was so not ready for the hot box.

As Petra gracefully exhaled out the window, those black-mani'd fingers came pinching at the joint again, and pulled it away.

"Um, maybe keep it to one hit for now," Petra suggested, reaching for the roach lest Janie should cough up a lung this time.

"Why?" Janie snapped back. "It's not like I've never done marijuana before, Petra."

"No, I know," Petra lied. "It's just that . . . this bud is pretty brutal. It might be different from what you're used to."

"Thanks for the warning, Mom!" Janie mocked, and took another defiant toke. Petra narrowed her tea green eyes, confused. *Who was this megabitch hogging her weed, and what had she done with sweet little Janie Farrish?*

Petra and Janie waited in line behind two impossibly gazelle-like model types, who either were twins or had the same plastic surgeon.

"So Pet," Janie began, staring straight ahead, "are you gonna, like, tell everyone I didn't know how to smoke pot?"

"What? No," Petra replied.

Janie turned and narrowed her murky gray eyes at Petra like she wasn't convinced, and then nodded. She handed five bucks to a highly perforated bouncer and flashed him the inside of her wrist, which he proceeded to stamp with a giant smiley face. Without even looking back at Petra, Janie charged into the crowd, stomping in her knee-high boots.

Petra, perplexed and highly creeped out, handed a crumpled fin to the bouncer and offered him the inside of her milky white wrist. He slammed a giant happy face on to it. *Welcome to the weirdest night of your life,* Petra thought to herself.

Paul Elliot Miller was wearing what could only be described as a onesie. It had a hood attached to a zip-up sweater thing attached to pants. Thankfully, it had no feet. On his feet, instead, Paul wore Birkenstocks. His neck was dripping in necklaces from the Venice boardwalk, all of them adorned with massive blown glass beads. One of the beads had a tiny mushroom encased inside. Petra was overcome by the unfortunate urge to hide.

Paul stood off to the side of the stage while the rest of the band set up, shielding his eyes from the lights and trying to find somebody in the audience. He found her. Paul waved giddily and flashed Petra a peace sign. Yes. Her punk-rock prince, her badass beau, her death-metal dreamboat reached his henna-tattooed hand into the smoke-filled air, and he actually flashed her a peace sign. Petra did the only thing she could think to do: she flashed one back.

"Yo, is my sister on drugs?" Jake called from behind her. "She's acting like a total freak."

The freak in question was sidling up to the bar as they spoke, high on chronic and couture. Janie leaned on the edge of the bar while Creatures of Habit started in on their first number: "Adolescent Anarchy." Damn, she loved this song. Janie closed her eyes and began to nod and sway with the music. Wow, she was in a highly public place — and a highly awesome public place at that — and for once, Janie wasn't worried about what she looked like. Being stoned was awesome! Why hadn't anybody ever told her how awesome it was before?

Janie felt a tap on her bare shoulder and opened her eyes to find a ferocious-looking guy in a wife beater glaring back at her. "Oh, sorry," she mumbled under the blaring music, and started to move out of his way.

"Wait," he called, catching Janie by a lock of her silky brown bob. "Hi."

"Hi," Janie answered.

He had a cleft chin, sunken cheeks, and longish greasy hair; think Robert Pattinson after a bar fight. A tattoo of a cross peeked out of the stretched neck of his wife beater. Everybody at Janie's high school talked about getting tattoos, but nobody she knew actually *had* one, which made Janie think this vampirical stunner might not be in high school at all. His eyes were half closed, meaning he was either half drunk or wholly into Janie. Or both.

"You here for Nocturnal Hunger?" he inquired.

"No," Janie replied, "Creatures of Habit."

He nodded. "They're good."

"Yeah, my best friend is the singer." Janie glanced at the stage and found Amelia looking back at her while Paul fiddled with her amp between songs. Amelia gave a double thumbs-up, and Janie quickly looked away.

"So, you're with the band," the mystery man smiled, revealing a row of oddly appealing crooked teeth. Then he extended his clear plastic cup and asked, "Beer?"

"What?" Janie yelled. The bar area was loud enough that she could buy an extra minute of panic time by making him repeat himself.

"I! Said!" he yelled over the noise. "Do! You! Want! Some! Beer!"

Like Natalie Imbruglia, Janie was torn. On one hand, it was working! She had officially turned into the kind of person that tattooed older guys offer beer to like it's nothing. But on the other hand, what about her Accutane? Janie was on this insanely strong acne medication called Accutane, and one of its side effects was high sensitivity to alcoholic beverages. Wait, Janie realized slowly . . . *high sensitivity to alcoholic beverages?* Awesome!

She grabbed the cup and took a long swig of the frothy amber liquid. Then she smiled a syrupy smile and wiped the back of her mouth with her hand.

"Have some more," suggested her sexy companion. "I'll get another."

"Thanks," Janie nodded. "Cool."

"I'm Ezra."

"Janie."

"You're a fun girl, Janie."

Janie was floored. "What?" she asked.

Of all of the things Janie had been called in her life — smart, interesting, artistic, retarded — *fun* had never ever been one of them.

Ezra leaned in so his lips were almost touching her ear.

"I said you are a fun girl," he repeated, flecks of his spit hitting her neck in a way that should have been gross but actually wasn't. Creatures of Habit started in on "Death to Memories."

It was all so exciting. From the bumping bass to Amelia screaming "fuuuuuuuck meeeeeeeemories" to the flashing lights to the double thumbs-up, it was like Janie was the star of her own insanely awesome music video. She felt swirly and strange, sexy and dangerous. She felt invincible. Ezra was talking but she could not hear what he was saying and so she just smiled and nodded and laughed a hearty laugh and sort of swayed back and forth gently while she drained the cup of its frothy amber liquid. And she was feeling a bit woozy, but not necessarily in a bad way, and she was feeling like this guy was going to kiss her soon and she could already picture herself telling Amelia all about it tomorrow and how awesome that would be and how once and for all she would vault into the bracket of Amelia's cool friends and would forever leave behind her old label as Amelia's sort of quirky little inexperienced buddy. So Janie just had to keep smiling and laughing and letting Ezra talk and soon he was going to kiss her. It was so obvious. And now he was taking her hand in his and flipping it over and saying something about her palm and she was sort of swaying backward on her five-and-a-half-inch heels and then for whatever reason — God only knows why — *he* popped into her head.

Evan.

Evan in the projection room.

Janie let herself relish the memory for a second, of how he had hooked his thumb over the waistband of her jeans so his finger was touching the right-above-her-butt skin . . . *Snap out of it!* Janie tried to focus on Ezra, who was tracing the lines on her palm with his own finger now and gazing at her through a curtain of ink-black lashes. He was close now. Slow-dance close.

Evan flashed into Janie's head again, this time by Melissa's pool, that first gentle kiss, before it had gotten truly Frenchy, when her lips had just locked with his in this extended peck. No! Stop obsessing. New Janie didn't waste her precious time reliving the past. New Janie was so busy and fabulous that she didn't even *remember* the past. And New Janie sure as heck did not sit around yearning for some board-shorts-sporting surfer dude. She liked the dark and brooding, tortured artist types. The Paul Elliot Millers and Ezras of the world.

"Are you okay?" Ezra asked. "You look like you're gonna cry or something." Janie stared up at him, in all his greasy inked-up glory, and smiled.

"Beyond okay," she lied.

'Cause Amelia was right. All Janie needed to do in order to forget about Evan was to replace him with somebody new. As soon as Janie locked lips with What'sHisFace here, the Evan spell would break, and all of the Evan memories would just be washed from her mind, a la *Eternal Sunlight of the Spotless Mind*. But wait . . . didn't things turn out really badly by the end of that movie?

And right then, that cursed line started playing in Janie's head on repeat, like it had so many times that week: *She kisses like a dogfish? What the hell is a dogfish? She kisses like a dogfish? What the hell is a dogfish? She kisses like a dogfish? Dogfish? Dogfish!!!*

"Fuuuuuuuuuuckkkk meeeeeeeeeemories," Amelia belted out for the final time, and Janie squeezed her eyes shut and leaned forward. Ezra took the signal, and before she knew it, his pierced tongue was searching the inside of her mouth, tasting of cigarettes, stale beer, and broken dreams.

The audience went berserk.

"Show's over, bitches!" Amelia bellowed into the microphone while Janie regained her footing. Ezra leered at her, hungry for more.

His face had changed to something famished, insatiable. He reached for Janie's slender waist and pulled her toward him, way closer than slow dance close. With her entire body pressed against his entire body, Janie was overcome by a wave of nausea; an overwhelming, all-encompassing desire to yak. Janie had no clue if it was from the dirty-gym-socks taste of this guy's tongue or the feeling of his scrawny body entwined with hers or those two huge hits of weed in the Volvo before the concert or the empty cup of beer in her hand that had once been full or the image of clean, pristine, and unbearably beautiful Evan that was welling up in her mind anew now and obviously had not been exorcised through her deep-throated makeout sesh with the very excited and very scary person holding her against him in a death grip. God, he was strong for his size. Janie closed her eyes, this time not to invite another throat excavation but to make the spinning stop. But Ezra didn't know that. And so he leaned in to lay another one on her — and he would have too, if some insane blond hippie chick hadn't busted in.

"Hey!" Petra squawked, and snatched her teetering pal away from the lascivious stranger. "What's with you, dude? Can you not see how wasted she is?"

"Hold up," corrected Ezra, "*she* kissed *me*." Then he added, skeezily for Janie's benefit, "And she knows what she's doing."

But just as Petra prepared to give the butt-chinned cree poid a piece of her mind, she heard her name come through the speakers. Petra turned to find her onesie-clad beau standing alone on the stage.

"Petra Greene," Paul repeated into the mic, staring at her and causing everybody else in the room to do the same, "this one's for you."

Paul's declaration was met by a swell of applause from the audience, peppered with deep grunts and high-pitched wails. Creatures of Habit was doing an encore! Or so they thought . . .

Paul pulled out a pan flute and held it to his perfect pink lips. He then proceeded to daintily blow into the bamboo tubes, producing a sound reminiscent of a Renaissance fair. As Paul slid up and down the instrument, Petra watched, horrified. Then somebody behind her said what everybody in the room was thinking. . . .

"Boo!"

Paul kept playing, either unaware of or indifferent to the tidal wave of boos steadily mounting in the audience below.

"Go back to Narnia, you freak!" someone bellowed.

"Let's get out of here," Petra demanded. A woman could only endure so much. She jostled Janie (the only person in the room who had been soothed to the point of falling asleep standing up by Paul's pan flute solo) while the notes continued to tinker like wind chimes on a breezy afternoon.

"Petra Greene?" called a voice behind them. Petra turned, and a chubby kid with a septum pierce promptly chucked his entire beer in her direction. Petra gasped, disbelieving — though only slightly sprayed — and then turned to see where the bulk of the bevy had landed; Janie was drenched.

"Way to go, you jackass *Yoko*," spat the angry punk.

"You little shit!" wailed Petra, wresting herself away from Janie and lunging toward the little jerk. He sprinted away, cackling like a wicked fairy, but Jake appeared out of nowhere and tripped him, sending the evil imp flying.

"Let's get out of here," Jake advised, scooping his sloppy sister onto his shoulder and leading the way toward the exit. Petra was more than happy to oblige. The night had been like some kind of trippy nightmare, and she couldn't wait to wake up.

And Petra wasn't the only one horrified by the evening's events. Standing by the men's room while Jake, Janie, and Petra hightailed it out of there was an impossibly out of place blond kid with smooth tan skin and a sickly expression on his rose wax lips. How long had he been standing there? All alone in his board shorts and flip-flops? And what had he just witnessed that had left him looking so completely and utterly, incomparably appalled?

The Girl: Janie Farrish
The Getup: Trashed

Having never had a hangover before, Janie was stunned by just how bad it was possible to feel. When she had been sick in the past, it had always been an either/or situation. *Either* her head ached *or* her stomach was queasy; *either* her throat itched *or* her muscles throbbed. Today, Janie needed a fifth choice: all of the above. What the hell happened last night?

"What the hell happened last night?" whispered Jake. He had tiptoed into Janie's bedroom to check on her. And also to make fun of her for being such a mess the night before, of course.

"You tell me," Janie replied without moving from her facedown-on-pillow position.

"Well," Jake began, "from what I could ascertain, the party spirit of Tara Reid entered your body and possessed you for the evening. She smoked a bunch of Petra's weed, drank a huge beer even though she is on Accutane, let a Hells Angel grope her by the bar, and then came home and puked all over the bathroom, but with the help of her loving brother, her mom did not find out, and now she has agreed to give said loving brother the Volvo for the next two weeks in exchange for his vomit-cleanup services and continued silence."

"Fine, whatever," mumbled Janie. Just hearing the word "Volvo" made her carsick.

"Sweet!" Jake exclaimed, impressed by how easy that had been. He stood up and headed for the door. Janie flipped over.

"Where are you going?" she whined. "You can't abandon me in this state." The mere act of rolling onto her back made Janie's head throb like it was stuck in a vise. She squeezed her eyes shut. "Ow!"

"What!" Jake exclaimed.

"My head!"

Jake laughed. "Tara Reid left you with one wicked hangover." He opened the door.

"Jake!" Janie wailed. "Seriously, where are you going?"

"I have to go to Charlotte's," he said, pulling a loose thread from the hem of his vintage cowboy shirt and watching it unravel. "She wants to 'talk,' and I'd rather get it over with now than postpone the inevitable."

"Which is . . . ?" his invalid sister inquired.

Jake sighed. "Every time Charlotte says she 'wants to talk,' it really means she wants to interrogate me about Dogfish again. And then tell me she's not ready to get back together."

Janie popped up to sitting, despite her head spins. "Dogfish?" she gasped.

"It's our nickname for Nikki Pellegrini. Charlotte is still

obsessing over that stupid kiss, so I told her kissing Nikki Pellegrini was disgusting. That she kissed like a dogfish. Which, in retrospect, was not a very considerate thing to say, since I have never kissed a dogfish before and maybe they are actually very skilled in the—"

"What!" bellowed Janie. "Nikki Pellegrini is Dogfish!?!"

Jake started. "Wow, chill out. I know it was a kind of jerky thing to say, but I just wanted to make Charlotte feel better."

Janie's heart was racing; practically bouncing out of her chest. She had broken things off with Evan — *darling Evan!* — over something he had never even said about her. She had squandered their incredible connection over something that had never even happened, and now he probably completely hated her. She'd ignored his texts, ditched their date . . . oh God! She'd made out with that disgusting walking cigarette butt at the concert last night.

"I'm coming with you to Charlotte's," Janie announced, tearing back the covers. "I have to talk to Evan."

"Eew! Eew-eew-eew-eew-eew!" wailed Jake as he turned onto Charlotte's tree-lined street. "That's like, incest!"

"How is that incest?" Janie rejoined from the passenger

seat. Jake had refused to take Janie with him to Charlotte's unless she told him why she wanted to go so badly, and so finally she'd just spilled it all: how she'd hooked up with Evan, how she'd overheard Charlotte talking to Jake and thought she was talking to Evan, and how she'd dissed Evan — the guy of her dreams — over a stupid misunderstanding. She'd wanted Jake's sympathy. But instead, what she got was . . .

"Eew!"

"Yes, I heard you the first fifty times," Janie replied.

"You cannot date Evan if I am dating Charlotte," Jake shuddered.

"Well, lucky for me, then, Charlotte doesn't want to date you," Janie quipped. "Can you drive any slower, Grandma?"

Jake gripped the steering wheel so hard his knuckles turned white.

"So, did you not even consider the grossness of swapping siblings before entering into this romance with my girlfriend's brother?" Jake inquired. *In truth?* Janie thought. *Not really.* She had been way too busy worrying about Evan being Charlotte's brother to get around to worrying about Charlotte being Jake's girlfriend.

"If you say anything to Charlotte I will kill you," Janie warned. "She's already done enough damage."

"Why would I say anything to Charlotte? If she knows my sister is shacking up with her brother then she *really* won't want to date me." Jake winced. "If *you* say anything to Charlotte, I'll kill *you*."

"Don't worry about that," Janie replied, gnawing on her thumbnail till she chipped the perfect black polish. Janie flapped the passenger side mirror down and stared at her reflection. Her skin looked blotchy, and somehow dry and oily at the same time. Her eyebrows were actually tangled. Janie didn't even know eyebrows could get tangled. Her bangs, which had fallen in a perfect glistening curtain when she'd left the house the night before, had devolved into a row of greasy wisps, parted in the middle. She tried to comb them down over her forehead with her fingers, but the oily stands refused to form a cohesive whole. She grabbed two bobby pins out of the cup holder that served as her portable beauty shop and pinned the scraggly strands back to the rest of her hair. No better. No worse. Janie stared at her bedraggled reflection and marveled at her own stupidity. It seemed so obvious now. Of course Charlotte was still obsessing over Nikki Pellegrini. Of course she had been covering up when she told Janie she was on the phone with Evan. Of course Evan would not discuss Janie's makeout skills with his sister. It had all been a hideous misunderstanding. That much was certain. Now the only question was whether or not Janie could make it right again.

The Girl: Charlotte Beverwil
The Getup: Brown herringbone dress by Ralph Lauren
Blue Label, beige cashmere capelet by Giorgio Armani,
cranberry beret by M Missoni, raspberry ballerina
flats by Elizabeth and James, manicure (in Essie's
"Mademoiselle")

Charlotte answered the door in a capelet. A freaking capelet. And at the sight of her perfect glossy curls, her perfect
glossy lips, her perfect glossy nails — even her teeth were
glossy — Janie was overcome by the urge to mash her china
cup face in.

"Janie!" gasped Charlotte, taking in the beer stain on
Janie's ocean blue bustier, the torn hem of her brand-new
mini, the knee-high stilettos, and the smeared mascara.
"Let me guess . . . you are going to the 'Thriller' tribute at
Staples?"

Janie wanted to strangle Charlotte with her cashmere
capelet. But instead she announced, "I need to talk to
Evan."

"He's not here," Charlotte replied. Jake strolled up the
combed gravel drive and met them at the door to the Beverwils' 8,000-square-foot Spanish colonial estate. "Hello,
Jake," Charlotte intoned, kissing him once on each flushed
pink cheek. "Come in."

Jake strolled into the house, headed for Charlotte's sprawling candy-colored bedroom. "Catch ya later, Courtney Love," he called to Janie.

"Where is Evan?" Janie asked.

"Why?" Charlotte inquired. "Are you, like, obsessed with Evan? That's so cute!"

But Janie did not have time to cook up an excuse — or to give Charlotte a black eye — and so she grabbed her copy of the Volvo key out of her ratty hobo and bolted back down the long gravel drive.

"Tell Jake I said sorry," Janie called behind her. Jake would have to find his own way home. Janie had to take the car. She had to find Evan. But if he wasn't home, where could he be? There was only one place Janie could think to look. Something inside her said that's where he would be, but how could she be sure? Janie had been (oh so) wrong about Evan before. She started the engine and hoped for the best, placated by the fact that at the very least, things couldn't get much worse.

It was one of those overcast late afternoons inching into early evenings in Santa Monica that leave the beach all but empty. A slumbering homeless man on a bench and one lone Rollerblader were all Janie could see as she swept the Volvo into the parking lot in front of Station 26, the only place she could think to look for Evan. He'd told her once that he liked to go there to think. And also when he didn't want to think. When he just wanted to clear his head. It was a throwaway comment, but Janie remembered it clearly. And everything else Evan had ever said to her, for that matter. Janie leaped from her vehicle and slammed the door, click-clacking toward the beach in her scuffed Louboutins. She reached the sand, pulled off her boots and socks, and ran toward the lifeguard station in her bare feet. In the murky gray late afternoon light, the station was just a blur. But as Janie padded closer and closer, it slowly came into focus, and as it did, so too did the sandy-haired boy sitting on the edge of the platform, letting his long legs dangle off the edge, and staring into the endless ocean before him.

"Evan!" Janie cried, sprinting toward him like she might miss him if she didn't run as fast as her bony legs could carry her. She probably looked like a hooker the morning after, in her unraveling, cigarette-burned miniskirt and beer-stained bustier, but Janie did not care. She had to get to Evan. She had to explain. *Now!*

"Evan!" she called again. This time he turned, but Janie could not make out his expression. Finally, out of breath, she reached the foot of the lifeguard station, huffing and puffing to regain her composure.

"What are you doing here?" Evan asked.

"I have to talk to you," Janie announced. "Can I come up?"

Evan stared into the ocean and mumbled something.

"What?" Janie asked.

"Free country," he repeated. Janie mounted the stairs and crouched down on the painted wood floor beside him, folding her bony legs beneath her and facing Evan while his chlorine green eyes remained trained on the water. Janie had never seen Evan at the beach before. It looked so natural. His eyes were sea glass, his skin was driftwood, his soft steady breathing was the tide itself.

"You are not going to believe this," Janie began, "but there has been a horrible mix-up." Evan remained stoic, unmoving. A salty breeze rushed past them and chilled Janie's bare shoulders. The sun was beginning to set, streaking the foggy sky with the murky golds and battered purples of a fading bruise.

"Evan, I know you probably hate me right now for being so flaky lately, but there is a reason for everything that happened. The other day at Ted Pelligan's, I overheard Charlotte talking to Jake about Nikki Pellegrini and how she kissed like a dogfish. When Charlotte got off the phone she lied and pretended she was talking to you, and so I thought that you had told her kissing me was like — well, you know — and then I was so hurt and insulted that I did not show up at the projection room or text you back." Janie felt like she could finally exhale. "How tragic is that?"

Evan turned to face her, his expression still empty. "So it was all Charlotte's fault," he said.

"Yes!" Janie exclaimed, relieved.

"It was Charlotte's fault you thought I said something bad about you, and it was Charlotte's fault you did not meet me in the projection room, and it was Charlotte's fault you never texted me back. . . ."

"Exactly!"

". . . and it was Charlotte's fault you made out with some guy who was old enough to be your father at the Creatures of Habit show last night."

Janie froze. "No — wait, what? Who told—"

"Nobody told me anything, Janie. I *saw* you."

The sky was the sickly smeared purple of a mashed prune.

"I can explain that too," Janie began, but Evan cut her off by laughing aloud.

"Yeah, I bet you can. It seems like you have an explanation for just about everything right now."

"I swear—"

"Listen, you don't have to get into it, okay? It's not like I'm your boyfriend or something. You don't owe me anything."

"I know I don't, or, you're not," Janie stammered, "but . . . just . . . what you saw? That guy . . . ? That wasn't me last night. *I* wasn't me last night. I smoked pot for the first time ever and drank some beer and . . . I don't know. It's like I was possessed or something. And to be totally, humiliatingly honest here . . ." Janie slowed. Was she really going to say this? Wasn't this conversation already mortifying enough? But hey, she'd gone this far; might as well go for broke.

"All I could think about all night was you. And as crazy as this is going to sound, I thought that maybe if I kissed somebody else it would help me get over my feelings for you. But instead, I woke up today feeling lower than I ever have, and not just because it felt like somebody was mashing an ice pick into my ear, but because kissing that guy did not make me miss you any less. It just made me miss you more." Okay, that was enough. Janie officially needed to stop talking now. She had said *more than enough* and now it was up to Evan to reply.

Evan stared into Janie's slate gray eyes like he was searching for something. His gaze was piercing, probing; she resisted the urge to avert her gaze. Finally, Evan turned away, shaking his head so his sandy blond locks shook in the icy air. The waves crashed loud and hard like a bookcase collapsing.

"Don't you believe me?" Janie pleaded. *Talk about groveling,* she thought. *This was unbearable. What more did he want her to say?*

"Do I believe you?" Evan pondered, staring out at the

murky horizon. He shrugged. "I don't really know anymore." Janie was broken. How could she make Evan understand that it was all just a horrid misunderstanding? That she had never meant to hurt him? That she had never even thought she *could* hurt him?

"Please," Janie begged, hearing the telltale quiver in her voice that meant she was probably going to cry soon. Oh God. She really, really did not want to cry right now. "Tell me what I can do to make things normal again," she whispered.

"You know," Evan replied, "I think you've done enough already." A lump rose in Janie's throat. So that was it? It was all just over? Because of something *he* never said and something *she* never meant to do?

"But I like you!" Janie wailed.

"I like you too." Evan nodded. "I *liked* you."

It was the first time Evan had ever told Janie he liked her. And it was already over.

"Liked?" Janie repeated. Evan let out something like a growl. Like he was holding in a fury that could consume him completely if he wasn't careful. He cracked his knuckles and then his neck and took a deep breath. He balled his hands into fists and then stretched them out again.

"I just" — Evan looked down at his lap and shook his head — "I need to think. I can't handle this right now."

He didn't even say good-bye. Evan rose and walked back

down the ladder, keeping his beautiful face trained on the steps all the way. Then, he left. He just started walking across the sand toward the parking lot, alternately shaking his hands out at his sides and running them through his tangled hair. At one point, he kicked the sand hard, and it spewed up in front of him like a desert geyser. Then he quickened his pace. Soon, Janie could not see him at all. He was gone. Evan was gone. Janie had lost him forever.

If the traffic light on the corner of Ocean Avenue and Pico Boulevard changed from red to green, and Janie had not given in and cried yet, Evan would call her. Janie trained her gaze on the light, feeling the growing burn behind her eyeballs but refusing to let the dam break. The light changed. She checked her cell phone. Nothing. Okay. That was okay. She could do it again at the next light. And the next light. And the next light. And one of those times it was bound to work. She just wasn't trying hard enough. She just wasn't believing enough. If Janie could truly believe that Evan would call, then she could make him call. Janie had read *The Secret*. She knew all about the Law of Attraction, capital L, capital A. Believe it and it is so. Imagine it and it will be. And so Janie kept on believing happy things. As hard as she could. While she inched down Ocean Avenue, catching every single red light.

Evan is my boyfriend, she envisioned. *He takes me surfing sometimes after school and I am really bad at it but he thinks it is just adorable. I get my first tan. And sometimes we just sit on our boards out there in the surf until the sun sets while the waves lap past us, talking about everything that has ever happened to us and laughing so hard and kissing each other even harder and feeling like there was never a time before the two of us were an "us." And we look back on that day at the lifeguard station when he told me he needed "to think" and walked away as the saddest day of either of our lives, and we are both so traumatized by that memory that we never spend a minute apart again. Okay, maybe a minute, but not much more. And Evan decides to get one of my drawings tattooed on his bicep — no, on his back? Yeah, on his back, and on my seventeenth birthday he tells me he loves me; that he has always loved me. And I don't say it back yet but I feel it too. And all of this joy and love and general awesomeness begins today — just moments from now — when I arrive at my house and Evan is sitting on my porch just waiting for me. (I'm not sure how he finds out where I live . . . maybe Charlotte tells him?) And when I walk up to him, Evan looks at me all hard at first and says, "Janie, don't you ever let another guy touch you again." And I am scared by the gruffness in his voice and the fire behind those pool green eyes, and I gulp and say, "Never." And he says, "Ever," or something sort of like that but better — in his own words, you know? — and then he reaches for the back of my head and just tears me toward him, wrapping me in that sandy salty strong embrace and I just relax into his body like I did that first time on the lawn and that second time in the projection room and then he kisses me hard, like a promise. And I surrender into him now and forever.*

Janie sighed. That was fun!

She idled at the crosswalk on Ocean Avenue and San Vicente Boulevard, waiting for a pair of joggers to pass. Her cell phone beeped. It was him . . . it had to be him! Janie took a deep breath and exhaled, relishing the sweet moment before her love story began in earnest. She rolled down her window and smiled, prolonging the agony that preceded the soon-to-be-glorious moment when she read what was sure to be Evan's text. Okay, so he hadn't shown up on her doorstep. Wasn't texting really the doorstep of 2010 anyway? Janie turned on the radio. Natasha Bedingfield. Cheesy, yet oddly apropos. *Feel the rain on your skin no one else can feel it for you only you can let it in no one else no one else . . .*

When Janie could not take the suspense any longer, she reached for her scuffed navy Samsung and popped it open.

It was Jake.

Charlotte and I got back together!

The dam broke.

And once it did there was no turning back. It felt so good to cry. Hot salty tears came streaming out of Janie's eyes, leaving trails down her dry blotchy cheeks and splattering on her bare arms and stained bustier. Snot or something like it came flooding from her nose; it was as if somebody had turned on a faucet in Janie's face and everything just came gushing out. It felt so fitting. After all, Janie was filthy. Had not even brushed her teeth that morning and still in those horrid clothes from the night before. Why not be covered in snot and tears to complete the look? Janie wanted to rip her own hair out too, rip her clothing to shreds, rip the steering wheel clear out of the car.

She kept driving, taking side streets home instead of the far more expedient freeway. Janie wanted to prolong her misery; to wallow in it; to drown in it. She did not want to go home yet. What was waiting for her at home? Just her brother maybe, all glowing and giddy after reuniting with the midget bitch who had ruined Janie's life; and Janie's mess of a room, still chaotic from her excruciatingly involved primping session the night before; and her mom. Oh God. Janie really could not handle seeing her mom right now. The sorry state of her room would be enough to invoke the Wrath of Mom; look what she was wearing!

How had Janie's life gone from so good to so irrevocably wrecked in just a few short days? Janie cried and gulped and cried and gulped, her weeping wails only interrupted by her occasional need to gasp for air so she could wail anew. It felt good to wail. Amazing. Janie wailed louder. And then she rolled up the windows and screamed. She gripped the steering wheel and screamed again, as loud as she could, loud enough to tear her eardrums tear her lungs tear her heart. And as she inched down San Vicente behind a shiny black Hummer, Janie watched a stream of spandex-clad bikers pass her in the bicycle lane, and a mother pushing a Bugaboo stroller down the sidewalk. It blew her mind. How could all these people just bike around, stroll around, and otherwise continue living their lives as though everything was normal, when as far as Janie was concerned, this day was good as Armageddon?

The sky opened up then, no joke. They'd been predicting rain for days, and now here it was. Pelting her windshield and giving the Volvo its first wash in months. Janie turned on the windshield wiper and it made a horrible scraping sound as it swung back and forth across the glass. The rubber squeegee part had slid back in its track like it always did, leaving the metal wiper tip to scrape the windshield repeatedly, like nails on a chalkboard. Janie turned the wiper to a slower speed, and the sound improved slightly, but rain was pelting the windshield so hard then that she couldn't see a thing with the wiper on low. Plus, the tears streaming from her slate gray eyes — still, and with no signs of abating — did nothing to aid her already obstructed view. Janie pulled into a gas station to slide the rubber blade back up the wiper. And to gather her sorts somewhat, before she mowed down a baby carriage or a pair of bikers. She leaped from her car and slid the rubber blade back up the wiper like she had so many times before, and quickly got soaked in the process. Janie could not help but laugh. It was so bad it was funny. *What else you got? Lay it on me!* she felt like screaming to the man upstairs.

Janie got back into the car, slammed the door, and checked her phone. One text message. She inhaled, exhaled, pressed the read now button.

Jake again.

!!!

Janie started the Volvo and headed home.

The problem with driving is, no matter how many red lights you hit, no matter how many miles below the speed limit you drive, no matter how many ill-advised side streets you take, eventually, inevitably, you reach your destination. And so it was that Janie pulled into the driveway of her boxy one-story house in the pouring rain that Saturday at 7 p.m. She'd stretched the drive home from its usual forty-five minutes to an hour and a half. Now there was no place else to go. It was time to go in and face the music. Tear the Band-Aid off. Confront the Wrath of Mom.

Janie opened the door and found her mother waiting for her at the kitchen table, turquoise cat's-eye glasses down over her nose.

"We need to talk," Wendy Farrish announced.

Janie settled into the cracked vinyl chair across from her mother with peaceful resignation. "I know," she surrendered, "my room is a mess and I look like a waterlogged tranny."

"Your room is a mess?" Wendy inquired. "I haven't been in there. Please clean it up before the Patchetts arrive for dinner."

Shoot. She didn't even know about the room.

"So, if you haven't been into my room, then what did you want to talk to me about?"

Wendy paused. "I feel like Dad should be here for this conversation, but I don't think it can wait till Monday. Do you have anything you'd like to tell me?"

Hmmm, mused Janie. *That I have ruined the only wonderful thing that has ever happened to me? That I puked all over the bathroom last night? That I have not brushed my teeth in twenty-four hours and am starting to think there is nothing more foul in the entire universe than the taste in my mouth right now?*

"No," Janie replied. "Why?"

Wendy sighed, clearly disappointed to have to pull the information out of Janie instead of having her offer it up voluntarily. But Janie wasn't sure which information Wendy was even digging for. And she was not going to make the messy room mistake again. Janie peeled a bubble of Mod

Podge off of the kitchen table she had decoupaged with her mom years before. It was covered in pictures from *Teen Vogue* and *CosmoGirl*, along with words they'd cut out: *Rock-star, Flirt, Fearless, Daisy. . . .*

"Your credit card statement arrived today," Wendy announced, handing a folded sheet of paper to Janie. Janie did not bother unfolding the page. She knew what it said.

"Three thousand, four hundred eighty dollars," Wendy intoned. "Please tell me this was an accounting error."

"Nope, no error," Janie replied. "That's what clothes cost these days, Mom. Unless you want to shop at Walmart or something."

Wendy cocked her head, disbelieving. "I may not be the most fashionable mother in Los Angeles, but even I know there is no reason to spend that kind of money on clothing. What did you buy?"

"This," Janie answered. Wendy scanned her daughter's hot mess of an outfit.

"What else?"

"Nothing. Just this."

"Janie, what were you thinking?" Wendy fumed. "You know we don't have that kind of money!"

"*I* have that kind of money, Mom. From the Ted Pelligan deal. And so now, finally, I do not have to walk through the halls of Winston dressed like some kind of street urchin."

"Street urchin?" Wendy gasped. "Janie, what

happened to all those clothes we bought you at Old Navy right before school started?"

"Mom! You should never have even sent me to Winston Prep if you expected me to show up at school wearing Old Navy! That's like sending your kid to Iraq with a squirt gun!"

Wendy looked down at a well-shellacked Kate Moss cut-out and shook her head. "Those clothes are going back," she announced. "Today."

Janie couldn't help but laugh at that one. "Um, Mom, it's sort of a you-break-it-you-buy-it situation. I'm pretty sure they don't want these clothes back."

"Fine," nodded Wendy, "but I hope you really enjoyed your shopping spree, because that is the first and last time you will get to pull a stunt like that. From here on out, I will be placing all of your Poseur income in a trust until you are eighteen."

"You can't do that!" cried Janie. "That's completely unfair!"

"Yes I can, and no it's not."

"One day ago, you were telling me what a creep Petra's dad was for wanting to manage her money, and now you're doing the exact same thing! You're just as bad as he is! No, you're worse than he is, because you're being a phony about it, when all along you just wanted to control my share!"

"Are you done, Janie?"

No, she was not done! Janie was seething. What was

this, some kind of cruel joke played on her by some bitter god with a vendetta? What had she ever done to him? Or was he just bored up there in heaven and toying with her increasingly fragile emotions for sport? If so, she hoped he was getting a kick out of this. Janie's life had always sort of sucked and she was fine with that. She was *used to that*. But what she seriously could not handle was having the illusion of the perfect life — kissing Evan, the Teddy P. deal — and then having it all taken away from her as quickly as it had been given.

"Do whatever you want, Lady Farrish," Janie mocked. "Any other parts of my life you'd like to ruin while you're at it?"

"I would check your tone, young lady," Wendy snapped. "And this probably goes without saying, but just to be clear here, you are grounded."

The first thing Janie did when she entered her catastrophically messy, red-white-and-black-themed room was strip. She unhooked the suffocating bustier, shimmied out of the skintight mini, and then crouched down on her itchy red carpet in her day-old undies to survey the wreckage. There was no way in hell Ted Pelligan would take these clothes back. The bustier was stained with beer, the telltale red soles of the Louboutins were beyond scuffed, and the mini-skirt was unraveling at the seams. Not to mention singed with a cigarette burn. *Eew*, shuddered Janie. Was the cigarette burn from that slimy horndog she'd let grope her at the bar? And why had she let him do that anyway? Part of it was Amelia's fault, Janie decided, for encouraging the whole get-over-Evan-by-getting-under-someone-else approach, but Janie was pretty sure she could not blame the *entire* thing on Amelia. As much as she would have loved to.

Janie balled the garments together, as if mashing them into a tiny pellet could make them disappear, along with all the humiliation of the previous evening.

Her Samsung vibrated. *Oh great*, she thought; *now Jake and Charlotte are engaged.* Janie checked the caller ID: *Melissa Moon Calling.*

No thank you. In terms of people Janie could not handle talking to right now, Melissa ranked high on the list. Top five at least. Janie could just hear her stupid tinny voice: *Hay-ayyyyyy! It's Melissa calling to remind you how perfect my life is! My clothes are better than yours and my house is bigger than yours and my boyfriend is hotter than — what? — you don't even have a boyfriend? Ah-hahahah!*

The cell beeped with a voice mail.

Janie crawled onto her matted sheepskin rug, curled up in the fetal position, and dialed her voice mail.

"Hay-ayyyyyy!" called Melissa. "Janie, this is Melissa

Ebony Moon calling. Are you ready for tomorrow? Are you just so giddy you can barely walk? Me too! So, the shoot begins at two p.m. at the Standard Hotel on Sunset Boulevard. You cannot be late. Repeat: Can. Not. Be. Late. Y'all got me? And I know this goes without saying, but you must dress to kill, ma' bibble. That means no denim, no shoes involving laces and/or rubber soles, and obviously no t-shirts. Also, nothing that could possibly be construed as 'beachy.' Think Carrie Bradshaw on crack. Can't wait to see what you come up with! 'Kay, I am going to call Petra now and remind her not to show up in a burlap sack. Toodles! Oh — and Janie, if you have time, you might want to practice walking in heels in front of a mirror, 'cause, well, I've seen you wear heels before and . . . well, whatever. Just a thought. See you tomorrow! Hasta la pizza!"

Janie pressed delete, queasy. *Dress to kill?* How was she supposed to do that when Mama Farrish had put the kibosh on her spending? Janie headed for her closet, otherwise known as her only hope. Surely there was *something* wearable in here. . . .

But as Janie sifted through garment after garment, she soon realized her wardrobe was far from *Sex and the City*. At best, it was *Lizzie McGuire,* Season 1. In the front hung the few pieces Janie wore on a tiny rotation every day — Seven jeans, James Pearse tanks, vintage sweaters — and behind them hung a veritable wasteland of fashion backward pieces: a Hello

Kitty baby tee, some Wet Seal capri pants, a pinstriped vest from Forever21, a plaid schoolgirl skirt Janie had never worn, a cowboy shirt she'd stolen from Jake, a camo-print Hot Topic hoodie, some too-short Mudd jeans. . . . In the shoe department, Janie had her choice of Rocket Dog platform thongs, vintage bowling shoes, Converse she'd drawn stars on with a Sharpie, and Pumas with squiggle laces. In the life department, Janie had the option to kill herself.

She headed over to the matted sheepskin rug to curl up again. Maybe cry some more. But as Janie approached the rug, the matted ball of Teddy P. duds beside it caught her eye. And she could not seem to look away.

Balled up next to the furry, yellowing sheepskin, the rich blue velvet of the bustier glistened against the inky black cotton of the skirt, bisected by glimpses of shiny gold zipper, and a dog leash. Janie stared at the disparate fabrics until they melded together into a swirl of yellow and blue and black and gold.

And she got an idea.

It was entirely possible that it was an entirely terrible idea, but one thing was certain: Janie was not about to walk into the hippest hotel in Hollywood wearing a baby tee and Mudd jeans. She headed for her big red desk, where a pair of scissors rested in an empty Progresso soup can, along with some colored pencils. Janie drew in a breath and reached for the scissors' bright orange handle. . . .

The Girl: Petra Greene
The Getup: Silver ballet flats from Natalie Portman's tragically discontinued vegan shoe line, ivory Twelfth St. by Cynthia Vincent eco-friendly evening dress with dye-free taffeta ruffles, scalloped lace Free People barrette with beaded floral appliqué

The Girl: Melissa Moon
The Getup: Off-white Roberto Cavalli one-sleeve diamond-studded dress, vanilla goat leather Manolo Blahnik heels, diamond and gold cluster hoop earrings and bangles by Neil Lane

The Girl: Charlotte Beverwil
The Getup: Pleated persimmon blouse and aubergine/purple color-block taffeta skirt by Oscar de la Renta, black Valentino hidden platform heels, white Prada dress jacket, *The Stranger* by Albert Camus

The Girl: Janie Farrish
The Getup: Just you wait. . . .

Rudeness is an art, and the *Nylon* staff had mastered it. After all, they had studied under the best: *Nylon*'s editor in chief, Eric Snow.

When Snow — as everybody called him — interacted with the ladies of Poseur, he oscillated between vague curiosity and paralyzing disinterest. His frequent and untelegraphed mood swings kept everyone at the shoot — stylists, makeup artists, photographers — perpetually in awe of him. But the truth behind Snow's failure to focus was far simpler than any of his minions imagined; he was just crippled by ADD.

And also, he wasn't the sharpest stiletto in the closet. Snow could read parking signs and most menus, but that was where his linguistic abilities ended. Thus, Snow was more a figurehead for *Nylon* than an actual editor. The real editing was left to the ugly people. And Snow was far from ugly; more importantly though, the guy had style. While every other man in L.A. had gone the way of the tousled pompadour, Snow had started wearing his hair in a military cut, shorn close to the scalp on both sides, longer on top. His right eyebrow was missing a chunk in the middle, which he shaved off fresh each morning, and his glasses had only one arm, so they hung slightly off-kilter from his largish nose. During a recent one-night stand (who could remember which) a lover had stepped out of bed and onto Snow's glasses. Within the week, every scenester in L.A. was snapping an arm off his glasses.

"Snow," mumbled the remarkably disinterested woman reclined on the couch beside him. Her blunt black bangs obscured her eyes completely, if she even had eyes. "Time to shoot Poseur."

Bang Girl wielded the call sheet, and from what Melissa Moon could tell, her entire job consisted of reading it aloud to her semi-illiterate boss.

"Okay," Snow mumbled back (before sending off a BBM that read, "At standerd shot u cmon/?"). "Are they here?"

"Hello, Snow!" Melissa sang in response, plopping down on the edge of the couch. She tossed her Brazilian Keratin—straightened hair over her body-buttered shoulder and smiled big so her freshly bleached teeth gleamed against her LipFusion-plumped kisser. "Poseur will be ready to rock in five minutes. One of our designers had a family emergency and she is rushing over here just as fast as humanly possible."

Snow looked bored. As usual. "Okay," he shrugged. He slipped his BlackBerry into the pocket of his gray jeans, leaned his head back, and closed his eyes. *Was homeboy seriously taking a nap?*

"Great, thanks!" chirped Melissa, before scurrying off into the adjoining room, where all the designers being featured in the issue were milling nervously. The Standard had offered up two primo rooms to the *Nylon* shoot in exchange for some name-dropping in the issue. Not that the überchic Sunset Boulevard mainstay needed the publicity. Hollywood's hottest already swarmed there daily to languish in the palm tree—lined pool while big-name DJs spun the hottest tunes, unwind in the globe-shaped Lucite chairs that hung from the ceiling, dance at the windowless purple-lit lounge, and eat the famed burger at the throwback diner. And, of course, to gawk at the model who lay slumbering in a glass case in her underwear in the lobby all day. She represented everything the Standard stood for: beauty, sloth, and complete and utter indifference.

One person who was feeling far from indifferent at the Standard that day was Melissa Moon. Her brain was in overdrive, trying to figure out what to do if Janie did not show up soon. Janie had e-mailed the night before to say she was grounded and would have to sneak out to attend the shoot, but what was taking her so long? Melissa checked her rhinestone Sidekick again. Still nothing. Where the hell was Janie Farrish?

Melissa stomped over to the foot of the metallic beanbag chair where Petra was slouched, crocheting a bonnet.

"Hey Greene-bean," she whispered. "What am I supposed to tell Snow? It's two-thirty and Janie is still not here!"

Charlotte, who was sitting in the rotating wicker chair beside Petra, spun to face them.

"If she is not here in five, we go on without her. Just say she was never even part of Poseur. Say her name was just a big typo on the call sheet."

"A big typo," considered Melissa. "That's way harsh, Tai."

Charlotte shrugged. "*C'est la vie*. As long as Ted Pelligan doesn't tell Snow we're missing a girl, we can totally get away with it. And Ted is always late. Unless he gets here in the next five minutes, we're golden."

Melissa considered Charlotte's proposal. Dishonesty wasn't really her thing, but neither was squandering huge opportunities because other people couldn't get their you-know-what together. Melissa looked down at Emilio Poochie, slumbering soundly beside Petra's vegan ballet flat. He looked so chic in his Tiffany choker and rabbit fur stole. Melissa laughed inwardly; she had totally lied to Petra and said E. Poochie's stole was a fake. Why did fur get such a bad rap anyway? What was more natural than an *animal* wearing *animal fur*?

"Okay," agreed Melissa. "It is now two-thirty-one. We give her till two-thirty-six, and then . . . Janie who?"

"Deal," Charlotte agreed.

Melissa poked her patchouli-scented coworker's beanbag chair with the toe of her Manolo Blahnik goat leather heel. "Pet?"

"Whatever you say, Stalin."

Okay, so that was settled. If Janie did not somehow materialize in the next five minutes, she would be good as dead to them. Melissa felt better. But not all the way better.

Because she still knew that any minute, *he* would be arriving. Ariel Berkowitz, the nasty-looking creator of the even nastier-looking t-shirt line, Schizo Montana. Just knowing she would see his gnarly crooked grin in person made Melissa want to upchuck. Ariel's call time was two-thirty. Melissa knew that because she had checked the call sheet. And she had only checked the call sheet so she would be prepared to avoid him. Which is exactly what she planned to do. Like the fluorescent plague. Emilio Poochie leaped up and darted across the room.

"Emilio Poochie, no!" squawked Melissa. She watched Emilio bound across the shag rug toward the open door to the hallway. Then she watched him stop at a pair of leopard print men's tennis shoes and start licking the adjoining skinny ankles, wagging his tiny tail like he'd just eaten puppy chow.

"Hey little lady," called the owner of the ankles, kneeling to swoop up the fluttering furball. "Nice jacket," he laughed.

He cradled Emilio to his bony chest, where his t-shirt featured a photo of a homeless woman dancing on the Santa Monica pier. "Life's a beach," read the childish letters below the picture. Melissa felt ill. It was him. Ariel Berkowitz. And he was touching her baby!

She scurried across the room to the idiot in question, who was currently rocking Emilio like a newborn and rubbing his warm fat belly.

"What's your name, little mama?" Ariel intoned. Then he read the tag aloud: "Emilio Poochie. Oh, you're a dude?" He lifted the dog for confirmation. "You are! So how come your owner dressed you like a chick?"

Melissa stood before Ariel, toasted-almond arms crossed beneath her water bra—perked double-Ds. Ariel looked up and met her eyes.

Melissa felt a jolt of electricity zap her body. She blinked. *What the eff was that?* Maybe her new snake-venom supplements were kicking in?

"This little guy belong to you?" Ariel asked, and then he looked back down at Emilio and grinned that crooked grin Melissa had come to know and hate in the preceding week of cyberstalking. She set her jaw and reached out her arms.

"Dog," Melissa demanded. Ariel looked up at her, confused. And there it was again! When his eyes met hers, something pulsed through Melissa, threatening to erupt.

"Oh, sorry," Ariel said. "Here." He gently handed Emilio off to his seething owner. "I'm Ariel."

"Good for you," Melissa shot back, not daring to meet his beady black eyes lest she should be electrocuted again.

Ariel cocked his head to the side and squinted. "Wow, what's your problem?"

"My problem?" Melissa huffed. "I don't have a problem. Congratulations on the cover. I have always said there should be more mermaids in fashion. It really is discrimination that there aren't." And with that, Melissa spun around on her four-inch stacked heel, feeling fierce. But a slimy hand grabbed her by the body-buttered arm. She whipped around to face him.

"You're Diva Twelve or whatever!"

"I don't know what . . ." Melissa began, feeling oddly weak and out of sorts. Must be her new diet: sixteen small meals a day. Her system just wasn't used to it. Melissa felt like she was going to pass out. "I don't know what you are talking about," she finished, finally. She wrested her arm from Ariel's greasy grip, hoisted Emilio into the crook of her armpit, and strutted back across the room.

"I thought you'd be ugly," Ariel called as she click-clacked away. Melissa whipped around to shoot him a death glare, but when she did, she felt that damn feeling again.

Z-z-z-Z-a-A-a-P!

"Ted Pelligan is here!" hollered Nikki Pellegrini, whose job at the *Nylon* shoot up to that point had consisted of calling Janie, texting Janie, yelling "Janie!," and posting frantic messages on the wall of Janie's Facebook page.

"What!" gasped Melissa. "He was supposed to call when he was leaving the store. Where is he?"

"He just got out of the elevator and he's walking down the hall, surrounding by all these little yapping dogs."

"Oh my God, Nikki, he'll be here any second! Quick, go distract him!"

"Okay!" Nikki exclaimed. How?"

Melissa widened her eyes in disbelief. "Please do not make me go Naomi Campbell on you right now."

Nikki swallowed. "I'll figure something out," she chirped.

But just as Nikki turned to chase down Teddy P., the-man-the-myth-the-legend himself came barreling into the room, surrounded by a veritable fleet of papillons.

"My darling!" he bellowed at the sight of Melissa. The other designers turned to stare at the tottering man with the turquoise bow tie. He had to be somebody with an entrance like that. Emilio Poochie yip-yip-yipped at the approaching army of papillons.

"Emilio, shoosh!" scolded Melissa. "Hello, Ted," she smiled, and kissed him once on each round, ruddy cheek.

Upon Ted Pelligan's entrance, Charlotte actually deigned to rise from her wicker chair for the first time all afternoon. "Ted!" she exclaimed (careful not to lift her arm in greeting since she had a heinous streak of self-tanner there that she could not seem to scrub off).

"Hallo!" Petra sang, waving with her crochet hook from her comfy spot in the beanbag chair.

Melissa was trying to act calm, but inside she was having conniptions. If Janie did not materialize soon, they were toast. This was supposed to be Poseur's debut magazine spread, and one-fourth of the company was MIA. What if Ted told *Nylon* to call off the whole shebang?

But that's when Ted Pelligan said something that shocked Melissa and made her think that maybe they were going to be just fine.

"You all made it on time!" he announced. OMG . . . Ted had completely forgotten about Janie's existence!

"Actually—" Petra began.

"Yes, we did!" Melissa interrupted.

"I'm so sorry I'm late," winked Teddy. "Traffic was horrendous."

Cousin It Bangs materialized then. "Poseur?" she called from the doorway.

"Ready," yelped Melissa.

"Knock 'em dead," Ted Pelligan smiled. "And remember: hate the camera. Detest the camera. And it will love you. Try it for me quickly before you go."

Petra wrinkled her nose like she smelled something gross. Charlotte pretended to yawn. Melissa pursed her lips and acted pissed.

"Brilliant!" Ted exclaimed. "Now, go, my lovelies! I'm right behind you."

They all followed Cousin It Bangs into the other room,

where a rumpled California king was to be the set of the shoot. Could things get any cooler?

"So, the look I'm going for here is Hollywood Bad Girl," explained the black-clad Aussie photog. "I want you all sort of relaxing around the room the way you do when you hang out in real life. It should look like you just got home from a party together, but the real party is just about to start. . . ."

"Wait!" yelled a voice from the doorway. Everybody looked. Even Snow. There, standing in the doorway, was Janie, in the single most bizarre ensemble any of them had ever laid eyes on. The top was made of yellowish fur and studded straps, and the bottom was made of overlapping scales of black cotton and blue velvet, broken up by flashes of gold. What was she thinking? What was she *wearing*?

"What are you wearing?" gasped Snow.

"Pretend you don't know her," Melissa whispered.

"And who *are* you?" added Snow.

"I'm Janie Farrish," Janie announced, squaring her bony shoulders to the room full of incredulous stares. "I'm the fourth Poseur girl."

"It's . . ." Snow began, staring at the way the nubby fur bodice gave way to shredded velvet. The way the flashes of gold flecked the black cotton. "It's . . ."

Call Sheet Girl turned to Snow in disbelief. He was never this verbose.

"Art," he announced finally.

"Yeah, it is so beyond," cooed his black-haired lackey.

Ted Pelligan beamed with pride from his throne near the minibar.

"What is this creation?" Snow inquired, reaching out to touch the hem of Janie's crazy garment.

"I call it the Dogfish Dress," Janie announced.

"The newest design from Poseur!" Melissa rejoined.

THE
DOG
FISH
DRESS

Janie Farrish

December 26, 11:17 p.m.

Fellow Winstonians, Fashionistas, and Fabulazzi:

How's this for a Christmas/Hanukah/Kwanzaa/Festivus present? Poseur is not only gonna be in *Nylon*'s 20 Under 20 fashion issue, Poseur is gonna be on *Nylon*'s 20 Under 20 fashion issue! Yeah, you read that right. The painfully adorable Demi Lovato will be wearing Poseur's sick-ass new couture gown on the cover of *Nylon*'s February issue!

We here at Poseur would like to take this opportunity to say that we are oh so sorry to the creators of Schizo Montana for jacking the cover from them.

. . .

. . .

Okay, fine — y'all know me too well. We are SO not sorry! Ahahahahahaha!

So, since you are probably all itchin' to know how we edged out the mangy t-shirt dudes who were supposed to have the cover, here is the 411.com: Our photo in the mag was originally set to feature Poseur's now-infamous Trick-or-Treater bag, but Janie showed up to the shoot (way late, but who's counting) in Poseur's latest and greatest couture creation and the staff at Nylon went so bananas for it that they decided to change the whole plan. Trust me — I couldn't believe it either. Anyhoo, Poseur's new Dogfish Dress (it's capitals cuz it is that major) is like nothing you've ever seen. For real, for real.

The design was inspired by the sound your garbage disposal makes when something is stuck in it. Just-Josh-(Duhamel)-in! You know I love ya, Dogfish. The outfit is totally fab and although Farrish was the one wearing it to the shoot (and the one who gets a serious shout-out in the upcoming article), we all collaborated on the look. Don't get it twisted!

Aight y'all, I am off to celebrate — Bellinis or POMtinis? — so be sure to check back up on us at MoonWalksonMan soon. And if you are just dying to know what madness we are up to every minute of every day — you know you are! — follow us on Twitter, fan us on Facebook, and high-five us in the hall.

Happy ChristmaHanuKwanzaaVus (or something!) from your besties at Poseur.

Yours with a cherry on top,

Melissa, Janie, Charlotte, Petra

Welcome to Poppy.

A poppy is a beautiful blooming red flower
(like the one on the spine of this book). It is also
the name of the home of your favorite books.

Poppy takes the real world and makes it
a little funnier, a little more fabulous.

Poppy novels are wild, witty, and inspiring.
They were written just for you.

So sit back, get comfy, and pick a Poppy.

poppy

www.pickapoppy.com

gossip girl   THE CLIQUE   *the* daughters

ALPHAS   the it girl   POSEUR

THE A-LIST
HOLLYWOOD ROYALTY   SECRETS OF MY
HOLLYWOOD LIFE